Maybe This Time

an Oyster Bay novel

Olivia Miles

~ Rosewood Press ~

This is a work of fiction. Names, characters, businesses, places, events and incidents are either the products of the author's imagination or used in a fictitious manner. Any resemblance to actual persons, living or dead, or actual events is purely coincidental.

ISBN 978- 0999528426

MAYBE THIS TIME

First Edition: April 2018

Maybe This Time

an Oyster Bay novel

Chapter One

Abby Harper was just about to pull a tray of fresh blueberry scones from the oven when the phone rang. Again. She sighed, slung a dish towel over her shoulder, and, just in case some emergency had popped up, checked the screen.

It was Mimi, but then, of course it was. Who other than her grandmother would be calling her on Sunday morning? Her oldest sister, Bridget, was in the dining room at this very moment, refilling coffee mugs and tending to the inn's full house of guests. Margo, bless her, had chipped in to help with the crowd on the patio. Even little Emma, Bridget's nine-year-old daughter, was in charge of refilling water glasses. Carefully. Aside from a few friends and family members (who knew better than to call at this very busy hour), everyone in Abby's world was right here in this old house.

Well, everyone except for Mimi.

Eventually, the ringing stopped, and Abby was reaching for the oven door when the house phone rang. She shook her head, chuckling to herself, and, this time without looking at the screen, pulled the phone to her ear. It was the third call in fifteen minutes, after all. Not an emergency, though. If it was an emergency then someone on staff at Serenity Hills would have called her directly. Mimi was probably lonely or bored, and Abby hated to think of her like that. She much preferred to think of her here, in this sunny kitchen, mixing up muffin and cookie batter with a smile. "Good morning, Mimi!"

"Well, someone sounds chipper this morning," Mimi remarked in what some might call a snarky tone, but which Abby preferred to optimistically call a cranky one. In the background, Abby could hear the muffled purr of Pudgie, her grandmother's obese cat, who was forever within arm's reach unless he was terrorizing a visitor, in particular Margo, whom he'd never taken a shining to.

"I *am* chipper," Abby said, refusing to feed into the fact that Mimi didn't seem particularly thrilled by this. It made Abby sad, really. Until they'd moved her into Serenity Hills, the nursing home at the edge of town, Mimi had been like a second mother to her, filling the empty space and the hole in her heart every time she thought of her own parents, gone all too soon. But now Mimi lived in "a home" and she was clear to tell everyone it wasn't "her home." That they'd stuck her in it. That they didn't care. That they needed to bust her out and pronto.

"And what are you up to?"

"Oh, whisking up some eggs for a quiche," Abby said with a little less patience than she wished she could have. She cracked an egg into the bowl with one hand, the way she'd seen it done on her favorite cooking shows so many times, and reached for another. From the entrance to the dining room, she spotted Bridget, who was motioning to her to hurry up. Abby nodded, nearly causing the phone to slip from the crook of her neck. "Actually, Mimi, it's a bit of a bad time. Can I call you back later?"

"Later?" Mimi fell eerily silent. "Fine, fine. If I'm still alive later."

So it was one of those mornings. Mimi was feeling sorry for herself and nothing any of her three granddaughters could say would change her mind when she got like this.

"How is Earl this morning?" Distraction was always the best policy.

"He's *wonderful*," Mimi's tone changed when her special friend's name was brought up. "In fact, he's the reason that I called."

"Oh?" Abby wedged the phone tighter under her ear as she attempted to measure the cream. Bridget was still watching her, making arm movements to signal that she really needed something…something put on a plate? Back when they were kids growing up in this house, the girls would spend hours on rainy afternoons playing charades. Abby had never been much good at guessing, though, and Bridget had never been much good at acting.

"Last night, he asked me to marry him. And I said yes!"

Well, there it went. The house phone was now resting comfortably in the ingredients for the quiche, floating in a sea of whisked eggs, now coated in sticky yolk.

She fished the device out, wiped it off with the dish towel, and held it against her ear. It was pointless. No connection.

"Mimi?" Bridget asked with a knowing look. "She tried me three minutes ago."

"She's getting married," Abby blurted, even though a part of her regretted being the one to break the news.

News. No, this couldn't be true. Mimi and Earl had only met a little over a month ago, and then there was that whole business of him kidnapping Pudgie as a way to get to her attention...

"What?" Bridget's face was equal parts horror and surprise. "Are you sure she's not just confused?"

A sobering point. Considering the fact that Mimi rarely got her granddaughters' names straight anymore, this was a possibility. Abby set the phone down on a pile of paper towels, to deal with later. She'd have to start over with the eggs. "I suppose we'll know soon enough," she said with a sigh. "I'll stop over there later today and see what's going on."

"We have five orders for scones," Bridget said.

The scones! Abby flung open the oven and nearly whimpered at the sight. The edges of each were now tinged with a dark brown color that indicated they'd cooked a few minutes longer than they should have. Quickly, she pulled out the tray and set it on the counter, her shoulders slumping when she gingerly lifted one to check the bottom.

"I'll make a fresh batch," she said, cursing herself for answering the phone. She'd felt guilty, as a part of her always did when she arrived in this kitchen, the very same one where she used to stand with Mimi, who patiently taught her how to make a perfect pie crust, how to crimp the edges into a pretty ruffle. She'd go over to Serenity Hills. This afternoon. And she'd bring a batch of her fudge brownies—Mimi's favorite.

"They'll have to do. I can't make them wait for another batch." Bridget walked over to the range and inspected the tray.

Abby hated the unease that twisted her stomach into a knot. She wasn't a chef, not really. More like a cook, and a home-taught one at that. What she hadn't learned from Mimi, she'd gathered from cooking shows and recipe books and a *lot* of trial and error in what could barely pass for a kitchenette in her small apartment.

Bridget hadn't been exactly thrilled at the idea of serving food here; the original choice was for Harper House Inn to serve a continental breakfast only, and how boring was that, especially when Abby could offer so much more! So Abby had convinced her, worn her down, really, and now instead of serving fruit and pastries from Angie's Café every morning, Abby was whipping up French toast and quiche and…scones.

Only a few months into the arrangement, business was booming. Sure, the summer guests helped. Oyster Bay was a desirable destination for New England tourists, and Bridget had said the rooms were booked full until Labor Day. But now they had people coming just for Sunday brunch, people who were staying at the Oyster Bay Hotel, or even the smaller lodges on the shore. Even a few locals stopped in.

Still, things would slow down in the fall. Would Bridget still keep her on? The thought worried Abby every day, as did the "trial period" that Bridget occasionally referred to on days where Abby was a few minutes late. She knew she could just ask what the long-term plan was, but she didn't want to look like a charity case. Bridget felt responsible for her, after all. Always had. But then, Bridget felt responsible for everyone. Her daughter, her ex-husband, her new boyfriend, Mimi, of course, and even Margo, who was happily remarried and back in town to stay, with a successful interior design business and a baby surely in the picture someday soon.

No, Abby didn't want Bridget to feel responsible for her. She wanted…Well, she supposed she wanted her sister to believe in her.

Bridget pulled a few scones off the tray. "The ones in the middle aren't so bad. I'll take the best of this batch, and then tell anyone else who orders one that they're baking right now."

"I'm on it!" Abby said, reaching for a fresh mixing bowl. She didn't even have to refer to her recipe card anymore. The scones were a daily staple at the inn, made with Maine blueberries that every tourist (and local) claimed to be the best they'd ever tasted.

When the old scones were tossed in the bin and the new batch was in the oven, she returned to the quiche, hoping to make up for lost time as she cracked fresh eggs into a new bowl. She added a dash of salt, a sprinkle of pepper, and reached for the basil plant, only to see that she'd shucked the poor thing to the stems earlier that morning.

Good thing Emma had started an herb garden on Mimi's old vegetable patch as part of her school science project. Abby untied her apron strings and pushed out onto the back patio through the French doors. The sun hit her face and the salty breeze filled her lungs, and for one glorious second, Abby closed her eyes and breathed in, deeply, knowing all at once why she loved Oyster Bay, loved her home, and loved her life, especially these days, since she'd started working at the inn.

She wound her way along the wraparound porch that was lined with white wicker café tables and crisp blue pinstriped cushions. Margo was at the far end, chatting with a young couple about how they might spend the afternoon, and Abby gave her a little pat on the arm before she took the stairs down to the stone path that led back around the yard to the garden.

She had every intention of planting tomatoes here, already imagining how wonderful it would be to gather up fresh produce every morning before stepping into the kitchen. Sure, the market she frequented every Wednesday and Saturday was fresh from the farm, but there was something…romantic…about having it right outside your door.

She snorted to herself as she tore a few leaves of basil. Romantic. When was the last time she even entertained that word, truly?

A long time ago, she thought firmly.

With her herbs in hand, she stood, took one wistful glance at the ocean that met the edge of the property, and turned back to the porch…and right into the face of a man who was staring at her with far too much interest.

She caught the bottom step, managing to steady herself before she fell, and tried to make sense of what she was seeing, telling herself that it couldn't be him, it wouldn't be him, he'd gone away, never to come back.

But crap. There was no denying it. It was Zach.

He was staring at her, his blue gaze turning alert as his eyebrows pulled into a frown, as if trying to understand what she was doing here at all, even though he knew damn well that this was her childhood home and, hello, the inn was called Harper House, meaning the house hadn't switched hands.

But still, he stared. And she just stood there, like a fish, her mouth gaped and her eyes no doubt bulging.

In all these years he'd never come back. Been too busy, too important, traveling the world, covering all the big events, the stuff that mattered, because clearly she hadn't. And she'd grown comfortable with that, happy even, knowing he was gone and she wouldn't ever have to see him again. And now…Well.

She forced her mouth closed, licked her bottom lip, and let her gaze shift to her trusty bicycle, propped against the garage doors. She could be back at her apartment in fifteen minutes flat if she pedaled hard enough, and something told her today she could. Today, in fact, she might make it back in only twelve. There was a bottle of white wine chilling in her fridge. Who cared if it wasn't anywhere close to noon?

"Abby." She couldn't tell if he was pleased to see her or if he was just being polite.

She, however, was more certain of her own emotions. Zach Dillon was a part of her past. A part she had banished. And he wasn't welcome here.

"What are you doing in Oyster Bay?" On my porch, to be exact, she wanted to say, but refrained. Professionalism and all that other stuff Bridget had drilled in. "Did you know I would be here?" As soon as she said it, she regretted it. After all, why would he seek her out, now, after all these years? He'd been clear as crystal when he'd ended their relationship, and not even her tears could change his mind. "I mean, Harper House…" Hint,

hint.

"Didn't realize they turned this house into a hotel," he said with a good-natured grin. She gave it the stink eye. This was all a bit cavalier, all things considered. But then, time had passed. He'd moved on. And she... "It looks great. You look great, Abby." He smiled broadly, as if he didn't touch upon a hundred memories with that simple sentence. As if he hadn't hit a part of her heart that had remained untapped ever since.

She hesitated, not wanting to give too much away. A part of her wanted to boast, to say that, in fact, she was the chef, or the cook at least, of this fine establishment, but the other part of her didn't want to make it look like she only had the job from a family connection. She knew what Zach thought of her. It was the same thing her own family thought of her. That she was aimless and unfocused and couldn't commit to a path in life. Well, she'd stayed in Oyster Bay. Stuck by the people she loved. Didn't that count for something?

It was a hell of a lot more than he could say, after all.

"My sister owns the house now," she told him. "And the business. And I...help out." She waved the bunch of basil, lamely. "Are you in town for long?"

She hooded her eyes, so he wouldn't think she cared about his response, but she did, she realized, she did care. She wanted him gone. Today. Right now, in fact.

"Stopping over." He shrugged, not giving anything else away.

Sweet relief was instantly replaced with sadness she

hadn't felt in years. Sadness she hadn't allowed, that she'd closed off as easily as she'd closed off everything that could lead to it.

"I'm here for a project. Work stuff," he finally elaborated. "Visiting my family…It's been a while."

A while? More like seven years.

"Feels like yesterday," he continued.

Her right eye seemed to twitch. Felt more like a hundred years ago. A lifetime ago. "A lot has happened since then," she said tightly. She could point out a few choice details, but that would require chitchat, and he wasn't an old neighbor she'd bumped into at the grocery store. She didn't need to hear about his family—she knew them and had all her life. She didn't need to hear about his job, not when it was the reason he'd used for leaving her.

"That it has," he said, his smile dropping just a bit but enough for her to notice.

She should smile, she knew, offer him up more than the cold stare that she couldn't stop even if she wanted to. The man was a customer, after all, she thought, looking down at his plate. He'd ordered the quiche and a side salad. Fresh squeezed orange juice was still resting in his glass. He was dining alone.

Not that she cared.

It was then that she noticed the burnt scone. A mere bite was taken from it, the rest left to sit in the sun.

Right. Time to get on with it. She held up the basil

leaves, hating what a pathetic excuse they were. "I should probably get these into the kitchen before they wilt."

Zach's gaze was unnerving, the same deep-set, clear blue eyes that she never could read properly. "It was nice seeing you again, Abby," Zach said as she started to walk away.

She couldn't help herself, even though, professionally speaking, she knew that she should. She tilted her head and looked him square in the eye.

"Was it?" she said, and turned, away from the face that used to fill her dreams, once with plans for the future, and later, with memories she only hoped to banish.

Her heart pounded as she walked back around the porch, the basil squeezed tightly in her hand, the faces at the tables a blur. She made it into the kitchen in time to pull the scones from the oven, her hands shaking as she set the tray on the range to cool.

They were baked perfectly, and Bridget would be pleased. But for the first time since she'd started working here, all Abby wanted to do was finish her shift, clean up, and clock out.

"It's going to be a hot one out there," Margo said, coming in off the porch. Her cheeks were flushed and she was fanning her face with her hand. "Hey, was that Zach Dillon at the back table?"

Abby busied herself with chopping the basil. "Yeah, it was."

"You guys used to date back in college, didn't you?" Margo asked the question frankly, no insinuation or hint of suggestion, and Abby wasn't sure whether to be grateful or annoyed. She knew what her sisters thought of her love life. That she dated too casually, too frequently, and too halfheartedly.

If only they knew.

"That was years ago," Abby replied in what she hoped passed for a breezy tone. Her heart was still thumping in her chest and her eyes kept darting to the set of glass doors. Every memory she'd forced out was now rising to the surface. Every kiss. Every touch. Every laugh. Every smile.

Margo poured herself a mug of coffee and took a sip. "I wonder what brought him back to Oyster Bay."

Not me, Abby thought. Instead, she set the quiche into the oven and closed the door. Loudly.

Margo shrugged. "Well, better get back out there." Suddenly noticing Abby's expression, she said, "Everything okay?"

No, everything is not okay, not in the least, Abby wanted to cry out. And she could, maybe. If there was one of her sisters she could confide in, it would be Margo. Margo was the middle sibling, not especially bossy, friendly to all. But Margo would run and tell Bridget. Uptight, worry wart, eldest sister Bridget. And she was already in trouble with Bridget enough for the moment due to those burnt scones, thank you very much.

"Mimi claims she's getting married," she offered instead.

Margo's eyes went round. "At her age? To Mr. Bow Tie? But she's only known the man for a couple months! Not even!"

"I'm going to visit her this afternoon," Abby said, knowing neither of her other sisters would. They were busy, they had lives. Margo and her husband Eddie were house hunting for something "family friendly" and Bridget and her boyfriend Jack were taking Emma to play miniature golf. And Abby, well, Abby didn't have anything to return to but an empty apartment.

And a heavy heart.

*

Mimi was in her room watching a game show when Abby tapped on the door a few hours later, a plastic container full of freshly baked brownies (minus the three she'd eaten straight from the pan, because seriously, she deserved it) carefully balanced on the other hand. Not so long ago, she would have just let herself in, but now that Mimi had Earl in her life, Abby didn't want to be greeted with any, um, surprises.

"Come in!" Mimi said, her smile broadening as Abby gingerly poked her head around the door and scanned the room. No geriatric limbs entangled. No bow ties discarded on the Berber carpet. It was safe.

Breathing a little easier, she bent down to kiss Mimi's cool, papery cheek and set the container on the bedside table, right beside the picture of her parents, taken long before Abby had come into the world. She smiled at the photo, her chest squeezing as it always did when she stared at her father's smile, so young and full of life, and the way her mother was laughing beside him. For as long as she could remember, she tried to imagine what her mother could be laughing about. She supposed she would never know.

She shook away the cobwebs. She was here on official spying business, after all. Bridget and Margo would be expecting a full report.

"Double chocolate fudge brownies," she said, with a conspiratorial wink. The very recipe Mimi had taught her all those years ago, when it was just the two of them living in that big old house. Back then, her grandmother always let her lick the spoon, a tradition Abby may have practiced today in the comfort of her own kitchen, because, well, feelings and all that...

It wasn't every day that your ex stumbled not only into your town but onto your actual porch. And while the house might technically belong to Bridget now, it would always be home to Abby. To all of them.

"You always smuggle in the best stuff," Mimi said with a sly smile, glancing at the door, as if the deluxe nursing home were a high-security prison.

"I also brought this," Abby said, plucking the bottle of sparkling wine from her knapsack. "Since we're celebrating?" She eyed her grandmother carefully, trying to gauge the reaction, but instead of looking confused or nonplussed, Mimi positively blushed.

Abby felt a flicker of panic. So it was true.

"Mimi, are you really getting married?" She tried to imagine how that would even work. Mimi was well into her eighties and Earl was definitely close. And they both lived here, in Serenity Hills. Would they get a bigger room, or just shuffle down the hall for conjugal visits?

She didn't want to think about the details too much.

"Of course I am! That's what I told you, wasn't it?"

"But…But…" There were just so many things she could say. So many reasons she could give for why this was crazy and reckless. She studied her grandmother with a critical eye. "But why now, Mimi?"

"Why not?" The woman tossed up her hands. "Isn't that what you always say, my girl?"

It was, at least it was something Abby used to say, often, actually. But recently, she didn't take things so lightly. Now there was something at stake. Her job. And once…her heart.

"Why not?" Abby shook her head. "That's not a good enough reason, Mimi. How do you think Bridget will respond to that?" She gave her grandmother a warning look, but Mimi just jutted her bottom lip in response.

"Bridget was always too worried. Has her knickers in a bunch, that one. I'd hoped finding this new man of hers would…loosen her up."

Oh, dear. Abby stifled a sigh and, without a word, reached for the container of brownies. She really shouldn't, considering she'd already had three (okay, four!) but why not just go all in. A half dozen. The day called for it. So what if her stomach was already starting to ache a little? Might be a good distraction from the hurt in her heart.

"She just worries," Abby said, taking a bite and chewing it quickly. "We all worry."

"Not enough to worry about locking me up here!" Mimi huffed. Her eyes turned beady with accusation.

Because there was no good response to that, and because Abby really didn't need to remind Mimi about the time she left the oven burner on for an extended period of time, she proffered the container of brownies, smiling to herself when Mimi picked the biggest one.

"I guess I just never thought you were, well, interested in finding love again," Abby admitted. Her grandfather had died years before Abby had been born, and then her parents had moved into the big seaside Victorian to help Mimi with the upkeep. There'd never been a gentleman caller in all those years, or any mention that Mimi wished there might be.

"I never thought I'd find love again after your grandfather died," Mimi said now, her eyes taking on a faraway look. "He understood me in a way no one else did. In a way I didn't think anyone else could. I busied myself with you girls. And then your parents died and, well, I busied myself even more."

Abby looked sharply at her grandmother. She rarely spoke of that time in her life. Just like she rarely spoke of the loss of Abby's parents, either. Some things were better kept in a quieter place, Abby supposed. And some things were just too difficult to think about too often, she thought, glancing at the photo again.

"Looking back, maybe I was hiding."

"Hiding?" Abby frowned.

"From the feeling of loss that inevitably comes with loving someone." Mimi smiled. But Abby struggled to swallow the rest of her sticky brownie. She understood. She understood all too well. More than Bridget knew or Margo knew, or even Mimi. More than she'd dared to admit to herself. Zach hadn't been just one of the many guys she'd dated. Zach had been…Zach. And there had never been a replacement.

"But I forgot how good it can feel too," Mimi smiled, and for a moment, Abby had the horrifying sense that her grandmother was going to discuss her nocturnal activities, but Mimi just shook her head and said, "He makes me laugh. And that…feels good."

Abby reached out and squeezed her grandmother's hand. "That makes me happy to hear."

"I had a lot of years alone," Mimi said.

"But…you never felt alone?"

Mimi looked at her like she was crazy. "With you lot? Never! Still…now…being here…" Another pointed look. "Better late than never. Take it from me, my girl, don't wait as long as I did to open your heart." She patted Abby's hand before releasing it to reach for another brownie.

Who ever said that Abby hadn't opened her heart?

There was Chase recently, until he followed his band to Florida, and then she'd had her eye on that cute male nurse who worked up on the second floor...but he only had his eye on the female nurse from floor three...She'd tried to move on. But opening her heart...that was another story.

"I'm happy for you, Mimi." Abby said, hoping that her sisters would feel the same, especially Bridget, who would no doubt fret about a hundred ways this could all go wrong.

"Then open that wine."

Abby did as she was told and held up her plastic cup. "What should we toast to?"

Mimi paused. "To second chances," she said.

Abby clinked her cup halfheartedly. Second chances. Truth was that she wasn't so sure she believed in them. At least, not for herself.

Chapter Two

The alarm went off the next morning at five sharp, just as it did every morning since Abby had started working at the inn, but today, unlike other days, she was already awake.

It was silly, really, thinking about Zach all night long, when she hadn't thought of him in years! She'd gotten over it, put him out of her mind, even managed not to flinch when she saw his parents or sister around town, and then…Then he had to resurface.

Well, chances were that would be the last she'd see of him. Soon he'd be gone, covering the latest upset in countries she had never visited and never would. Oyster Bay had never appealed to him. Never been enough.

Correction: *She* had never been enough.

Yes, best to remember that. Painful as it still was.

Abby pulled her hair into a ponytail, locked the door to her apartment, and bounded down the back stairs to the patch of grass that almost passed as a yard, even if it was split between the six units in her building. She was on her bike in no time, the salty breeze rushing at her face as she turned off her side street and entered town. It was still asleep, really, aside from Angie's. Even though Abby had managed to convince Bridget to phase out the daily deliveries of croissants and pastries, Abby still eyed the establishment warily as she pedaled past it. The crisp, striped awning was as cheerful as the planters full of bright blue hydrangeas that flanked the glass front door, and through the large window, Abby could see Angie setting a basket of muffins in the display case.

There was always a fallback for Bridget if things didn't work out with the sit-down dining service, but there wasn't a fallback for Abby, not unless you counted dog grooming or babysitting or answering phones at the doctor's office. And she'd done all that.

No, she had to make this work. Long term. And she would. She'd do whatever it took.

With that, she grinned a little easier and pedaled all the way to the inn, pulling up the gravel driveway to park her bike at the back of the porch. The house was dark and quiet, and Abby slipped in through the kitchen door with her key, careful not to wake Bridget or Emma whose sleeping quarters were just off that section of the house.

Soon they'd live in the carriage house over the three-car garage, no doubt. Jack was living there for now since moving from New York City in the spring, and it was hardly more than a functioning studio, with a small bath and not even a mini-fridge for a kitchen, but they had grand plans to turn it into a proper apartment someday. Grand plans for a lot of things, no doubt. After all, you didn't uproot your life unless you were committed to someone.

Her mind wandered back to Zach and she pushed that thought right back out. Nope, not going there today. Not having a repeat of yesterday. Today was fresh. Today would be wonderful.

And really, she was happy for Bridget. Bridget deserved to find happiness, especially when it had taken her so long to get out there again. Soon Bridget would remarry. Margo was remarried. Mimi was remarrying. And Abby, well, Abby had never even been married!

Not that she intended to. No, she had this kitchen to think about, her food, and her recipes. It was all she needed. At least it had been, until yesterday. Now, well, now she couldn't help thinking about everything else she'd once wanted from her life...

"Good morning!"

Abby looked up, gratefully, to see her niece standing in the doorway in a pink princess nightgown, her blonde hair tousled.

"Good morning, Emma! It's early for you to be up, isn't it?" She glanced at the clock on the wall. It was only seven. Breakfast didn't start until eight.

"Art camp starts today, and Mommy never sleeps in anyway. She doesn't want a guest to catch her in her pajamas." Emma rubbed the sleep from her eyes and climbed onto a barstool at the island. "Can I help crack the eggs?"

Seeing as it was Monday, and the inn was busiest on the weekends, Abby was only cooking for half the house today, and she'd decided on a brioche French toast with fresh strawberries and mascarpone whipped cream.

"Even better, you can whip the cream," she told Emma, giving her a conspiratorial wink. Over the years, they'd grown close, and Abby cherished the times she was alone with the little girl, serving as her favorite babysitter, of course. They had tea parties, and pretended they were at the salon, and they did all the girlish things that Abby had enjoyed as a child, and some things that Abby was happy to teach her, like the pleasure of a mud mask, or the thrill of watching a movie with all the lights out.

"Let me do it soon so I'm not late for camp!" Emma said eagerly, and Abby felt her heart roll over just like it did every time she looked at the little girl. She was a spitting image of Bridget at that age, though back then Bridget had seemed so old and wise and responsible, unlike the playful Emma.

But then, Bridget had always been an old soul that way.

"Good morning!" And there was Bridget, already dressed and showered, of course, just as Emma had said. Her hair was pulled back, and her makeup was minimal, but she was still so pretty, Abby always thought. Whereas Abby and Margo resembled their father, with auburn hair and green eyes, Bridget was fair like their mother. Some days, Abby appreciated this even more than Bridget knew.

Bridget yawned as she walked over to the coffee machine and began measuring out the grounds. Abby made a mental note to make that the first thing she did when she arrived in the kitchen from now on. Bonus points never hurt, and it would certainly surprise and please her sister. "Did you get the paper on your way in?"

"No, I came in around back this morning since the house seemed so quiet." Abby popped the lid on a container of strawberries and poured them into a colander to rinse.

"I'll get it!" Emma said, hopping off the barstool.

Bridget laughed as the little girl darted out of the kitchen. "Will she always be that helpful?"

"If she's anything like you, then yes," Abby said, recalling the way Bridget always helped their mother dry the dishes or set the table, or sometimes, even helped Abby to clean her room when the mess overwhelmed her, which was often.

"Here it is!" Emma said, returning to triumphantly slap the newspaper on the table.

"What about the others?" Bridget laughed. She ordered three copies of the local paper each day, and five of the *New York Times* Sunday edition, so the guests wouldn't have to fight over their favorite section. Abby wanted to tell her this was archaic, really. Didn't people read the news on their phones or tablets these days? But she picked her battles, and getting Bridget to allow her to prepare one meal a day for the guests was the one she was fighting. Eventually, they might have High Tea...especially around the holidays...but she was still working up to that. Maybe by this Christmas, she thought, her heart speeding up a bit.

"Oh." Emma hopped off the barstool, with markedly less enthusiasm this time, and walked out of the room, not bothering to hide her annoyance at having to step away from the cream that was ready to be whipped.

Bridget shook her head as she opened the paper. "Didn't even last 'til her teenage years," she laughed, but then suddenly stopped.

Abby frowned at her sister's pinched expression. "Everything okay?"

Bridget's eyes were scanning the paper. She didn't speak for the entire length of time it took Abby to shuck the stems for an entire pint of strawberries. Finally, without a word, she turned the paper over onto the counter and tapped her finger at the bottom left corner of the "Around Town" section. "Someone reviewed our inn."

"What?" Abby grabbed the paper, her heart pounding as she quickly scanned the brief article. "Despite the idyllic beachfront setting and the peaceful porch seating under the eaves of the giant maple, the scones were dry and hard—" She stopped reading.

Her scones were never dry and hard. Yesterday had been an exception.

Abby looked back at the paper, wincing, and searched for the byline. Reviewer on the Road. What a lame pseudonym.

"Who was it?" she wondered aloud. "I don't remember anyone complaining." She dared to look at her sister, and her stomach dropped at the disappointment in Bridget's face.

Bridget pulled the paper back toward her. "I only sent out five scones from that batch, and two were to the elderly couple in room three. They ate every last crumb. I remember because I was surprised they had such large appetites." Bridget looked down at the paper miserably.

Abby studied her sister with growing dread. This was it. The one thing she'd feared. Bridget had taken a chance on her and she'd messed up.

"I'm sorry, Bridget," she said, wishing there was more to say. Bridget wasn't shy in reminding her how much risk she'd taken on by buying this place and transforming it into a business. She was a single mom. She'd left a steady job as a real estate agent. And she'd hired Abby. A home cook. And she'd only hired her after Abby had pushed for it, insisted she could do it, promised not to let her down.

"It's okay," Bridget replied, but her tone said otherwise. She was worried, and sad, and why shouldn't she be? Up until today they maintained a steady four-and-a-half-star average on all the tourist websites. "After all, it wasn't all bad. They did compliment the ambiance and the presentation."

But not the food, Abby thought, feeling her stomach tighten.

"I'm going to set this right," she said firmly. Her teeth clenched as she set the strawberries to the side and cracked an egg into the bowl. She didn't trust her shaking hands with a knife just now.

Bridget walked over to the coffee machine and filled her mug. Normally she'd ask Abby if she wanted one too, but today she seemed distracted, and though Abby was craving caffeine, she wasn't going to ask.

"What's done is done," Bridget sighed. "A bad review was bound to happen eventually. You can't please everyone."

A bad review. She'd caused them a bad review. Abby closed her eyes.

"You can't please everyone, but I can find out who wrote this and change their mind!"

"And what are you going to do?" Bridget asked. "Go down to the paper and demand a retraction?" She shook her head as she walked into the dining room.

Leave it to Bridget to think of such a brilliant idea. That was *exactly* what she would do, Abby decided on the spot.

*

Three hours later, and armed with a basket of perfectly baked blueberry scones, Abby arrived at the office of the *Oyster Bay Gazette*. She'd rehearsed her speech for the entire five-minute walk from her apartment, but now that she was actually here, hovering outside the nondescript glass door in the center of Main Street, she suddenly felt odd and out of place. After all, she couldn't exactly force-feed the reviewer, could she? And she certainly didn't need to draw any more bad press to the inn.

But she didn't need to be the reason her sister lost business, either.

And she certainly didn't need a reason for Bridget to let her go. Not when Angie no doubt never burned a scone, and certainly never would have sent one over to the inn in her crisp white bakery boxes if she had.

"Here goes nothing," she muttered to herself, and, blowing out a breath before forcing a smile she didn't quite feel, she pushed through the glass door with her hip, clutching the basket of baked goods in two hands.

A smiling receptionist that Abby recognized as the granddaughter of Mimi's nemesis at Serenity Hills greeted her when she walked in. Fabulous. She hadn't even opened her mouth and she was already losing points. Mimi and Esther Preston had taken an instant disliking to each other since Esther made a move on Mitch LaMore, a mere matter of hours after his wife's passing, and word at the home was that she'd winked in Earl's direction a few times, too. There was also rumor of a struggle over a dinner roll at Sunday supper one night, and now the women sat on opposite ends of the dining room, and Esther was on a waiting list for another room, further from Mimi's, preferably with a view of the courtyard.

"You're Esther Preston's granddaughter, right?" Abby smiled nervously, hoping that she wouldn't be punished for the sins of her grandmother.

"You're Margaret Harper's granddaughter!" The girl gave a conspiratorial smile. "They're quite a pair, huh? I'm Sarah, by the way."

"Abby." Relieved, Abby set the basket on the desk and held out a hand.

"What brings you in today?" Sarah asked pleasantly, and for a moment Abby was momentarily startled that such a nice person could be related to the woman who had, indeed, hissed at Pudgie last week while Abby was wheeling Mimi's wheelchair to the nail salon. (Yes, Serenity Hills had a nail salon. And a hair salon. And a nightly movie. So why did Mimi insist on referring to it as Serenity Hell?)

"I was hoping to speak to the restaurant reviewer," Abby said with more confidence than she felt.

Sarah's face pinched in confusion. "Our restaurant reviewer?"

"The reviewer? From the About Town section?" When Sarah still looked perplexed, Abby pulled the newspaper from her tote bag. "Here," she said, tapping the article she hoped to later burn.

To her utter disappointment, Sarah leaned forward and read the entire article. "Oh," she said, shaking her head, and then, perhaps connecting association after she glanced at the scones, winced and said again. "Ohhhhh. You work there?"

Abby stuffed the article back into her tote, out of sight. She would buy up every copy in town by day's end if she could. "It's a family business. So as you can see, I really need to talk to him. Or her." Damn it, she had already messed up. Now all she needed was said reviewer to overhear and take offense and write another bad review.

She actually shuddered.

Sarah bit her lip and batted her big blue eyes innocently, the very same way Abby had seen Esther do the time Mimi accused her of taking the last chocolate pudding cup. "I wish I could help, but I have no idea who wrote that. I only started working here last month and, well, I'm just the receptionist."

"Maybe you could ask around?" It was worth a try, and she was desperate.

"Those types of articles are anonymous," Sarah said, shaking her head.

"Anonymous," Abby repeated. Of course. In a town this small, their identity would be well known. Most folks were born and raised here, and with the exception of the seasonal families who only came for summer, there was little hope for privacy. "But surely the staff must know…"

Sarah looked apologetic. "They don't tell me much around here. The reporters keep to themselves. And I'm new…"

"You grew up in Bar Harbor, didn't you?" Abby tried to remember anything else that she recalled hearing from Mimi's weekly complaints about Esther. When Sarah nodded, Abby said, "Well, I'm happy to give you the low down on Oyster Bay." Not that there was much to tell, unless you counted drinks at Dunley's as exciting… "The summer is always the best time here."

"I'd like that!" Sarah brightened. "And if I hear anything about the reviewer, I'll be sure to let you know."

"Thank you," Abby said, wishing she could press for more. She looked down at her basket of scones, wondering if it was a wasted effort. "Try a scone," she said, inching the basket across the desk.

Sarah looked horror-stricken and shook her head firmly. "I'm dieting. No starch, no sugar."

In other words, no fun. No recipes to bake, no sweets to enjoy. No thank you!

"You don't get a cheat day?" Abby pressed, thinking of the time Bridget had dieted to lose baby weight after Emma was born. Her cheat days were epic and planned with a fervor. Reservations were made a week in advance, or she'd ask Ryan, excellent cook that he was, to prepare his most decadent favorites, the more cream and cheese the better. Dessert was served at every meal, including breakfast, and the few times Abby was on break from college and back in town, she noticed how on cheat day dinners Bridget devoured the entire bread basket, complete with butter.

Abby smiled at the memory. Bridget was human. Surely she'd understand that Abby was too. And all this would…pass.

Sarah seemed to contemplate the notion of breaking her diet. Abby thought she detected a drop of saliva gathering at the corner of her mouth as she stared longingly at the basket. "Well, I did skip breakfast…"

Abby's eyes fluttered with impatience as Sarah broke off a piece that would barely feed a mouse and brought it to her lips. "Wow, that's delicious!" she said, tearing off a bigger piece.

Good, good. Abby breathed a little easier. Sarah thought her scones were good, and even though it might be her hunger strike talking, Abby would take the compliment.

"Maybe you could share that opinion with your coworkers? Put these in the conference room for me?" Then, because she may as well go all in, she pulled out the card she'd stuffed into the basket: Compliments of the Harper House Inn kitchen. "And if you wouldn't mind propping this up…"

"Happy to help!" Sarah said eagerly, as she took a large bite of the scone, scattering crumbs all over her desk.

Abby knew there was no sense in lingering. She'd done what she could, even if it didn't feel like much. She paused on her way to the door, where the staff list was posted, and, with one quick look at Sarah, who was now reaching for a second scone, completely oblivious to Abby at this point, she pulled out her phone and snapped a picture.

She'd track down the person behind that review. And then, she'd win them over.

Chapter Three

Zach waited until Abby had left the office to enter the small lobby. His eyes slid past the basket of scones to the card that was prominently displayed. Compliments of the Harper House Inn, huh? A regular delivery?

He decided to find out.

"Heading out to lunch?" Sarah asked as he approached the desk. She was clearly eager to befriend the other new person in the office, but in the week since he'd started, he was careful not to show her any false interest. He hadn't dated—not seriously anyway—since college. Work kept him busy, and it wouldn't have been fair to tie anyone down when he wasn't ever in one place for long.

Or so he'd told himself.

Zach kept one eye on Abby, who was now standing at the corner of the street, looking a little lost, despite Oyster Bay's town center only being comprised of four square blocks, and the fact that she'd grown up here.

"I am actually," he decided in that moment, even though he had a sandwich waiting for him back at his desk. One of the perks of shacking up on his sister's couch was that she packed him a lunch every morning, like he was a schoolboy. Today's offerings were peanut butter and jelly on wheat. He didn't have the heart to tell her he hadn't enjoyed that combo since he was about ten.

Pretending to only just now notice the basket of food, he said as casually as he could, "Who ordered these?"

"Oh, no one ordered them," Sarah explained in a hushed voice. "Abby Harper brought them over. From the inn? They got a bad review this morning and I think she's hoping to change someone's mind…"

"Huh," Zach said, shifting the weight on his feet. "Well, it's already in print."

Sarah shrugged and brushed some crumbs from her desk.

"She was that upset?" Zach frowned. From what he knew, Harper House Inn was owned and operated by Abby's oldest sister Bridget—the sister who had always driven Abby a little crazy, accentuated by their opposing personalities.

"Well." Sarah widened her eyes, as if the rest should be obvious. "The review did call the scones burned and dry."

"What if they were burned and dry?" he countered. Wasn't that the point of journalism? To report the facts, not the fiction?

Sarah just shrugged her shoulders and reached for the

phone when it rang.

Without waiting further, Zach pushed out into the sidewalk and hurried his step to the corner, where Abby was already halfway through the intersection. He opened his mouth to call out, tell her to wait and let him catch up, but then thought the better of it. He could already picture her scowl, her narrowed green eyes, her pinched mouth.

Better to play it a bit more casual. Like yesterday could have been, if he hadn't been so caught off guard to see her.

Harper House Inn. Of course he'd known it was her family's place. Known it was Abby's childhood home. But he'd only seen Margo, right up until the moment when Abby suddenly appeared, in the grass, nowhere near as happy to see him as he'd been to see her.

She was turning the corner now, and if memory served him correctly, the only place around the bend was Jojo's. Perfect. His stomach was rumbling and he could use a break from the office for a bit. Jojo's made the best pastrami on rye north of Manhattan.

He slowed his pace as he approached the café, trying not to stare in the windows as he pulled open the door.

And there she was. Already seated at the counter, a menu spread out in front of her. There was a spot free to her left, and before he could stop himself, he slid onto the stool, picked up a menu, and, as if pretending to only just notice her, said, "Abby?"

She looked up, blinking, and then, as suspected, narrowed her eyes on him and then slid them back to the menu in front of her.

"I can move if you'd prefer," he said, even though he had no intention of doing any such thing. For years he'd avoided Oyster Bay almost as much as he longed to return, a part of him knowing eventually he would, and wondering how it would be when he saw her again.

Her gaze skirted in his direction. Her mouth pinched tight. "I'm not staying long," she finally said.

He grinned a little, taking it as an invitation, or the closest thing he would get. Progress, perhaps? Whatever it was, he'd take it. A moment with the girl who got away. A chance to defrost her, bring out the spirit in her he'd missed. And loved.

"Darn," he admitted, forcing her to look at him in surprise. "I was sort of hoping we could catch up."

Her eyes were round now, so round he wasn't sure she was going to blink again. "Catch up?" she said, loudly. "You want to catch up *now*?"

He frowned. "Is there a better time?"

"How about seven years ago? Or how about a phone call once in all these years?" She shook her head, muttered something under her breath, and smiled sweetly at the nervous-looking young man who had approached them with a pad of paper, pen poised. "I'll have the turkey club, extra bacon, with a side of fries."

"And you, sir?" The poor kid's Adam's apple seemed to roll in his throat.

"The same," Zach said closing his menu.

"Since when do you like turkey clubs?" Abby asked, sipping her water. "And I thought bacon gave you a headache."

Conversation. They were getting somewhere.

"People can change," he said with a shrug. The truth was he hated turkey sandwiches. Really, could there be anything more dull? But one look at the gleam in her eye told him he'd have to choke it down. There'd be other lunches. But maybe not other lunches with Abby.

"Are you implying that *you've* changed?" she asked pertly.

He shrugged. God knew he had, even if a part of him was still fighting it. "I'm here, aren't I?"

As soon as the shadow fell over her face, he wished he hadn't chosen that point to highlight. It was a sore spot for them that he hadn't come back to Oyster Bay, the reason that everything had shifted between them. The reason he'd lost her.

She cleared her throat. "Well, I've changed, too."

"Oh?" He sank an elbow on the counter and leaned into it so he could face her better. Her face was unchanged, almost remarkably so, and her hair was a bit longer than it had been. She was just as pretty, though, if not even more so. Time had a way of making those memories fuzzy, the details unclear. Now he stared at her lips, her eyes, the dusting of freckles on her cheeks. He swallowed hard, realizing this was all more difficult than he thought it would be. And he'd always known it wouldn't be easy. It was one of the reasons he'd stayed away, even for holidays.

That and because maybe a part of him knew that if he stopped running, and just came home, it wouldn't be so easy to leave again. Bouncing from hotel to hotel and living out of a suitcase was a lifestyle that only worked if he didn't allow himself to stop moving forward.

Seeming to sense his gaze on her, she shifted in her seat. "I have a career I love, and I'm settled. And that feels good."

Settled. Could he say the same now that he was back in his hometown, a sleepy village on the coast of Maine? Now that he was no longer on the move, constantly on the go, and positioned in one place? He wished he could, but he was still too restless. Now maybe more than ever. His mind was darting, like he was trying to figure out the piece of this puzzle. Was he right to come here? And where else would he go? And how long would he stay? And what was next? He always had a plan. Until now.

"What do you do?" he asked, finding it sad that he didn't even know. He kept track of her through his mother over the years—lighthearted conversations about happenings around town and developments with its patrons. Nothing too intense. He knew that once Abby had worked as a dog walker, and another time at a hair salon. It wasn't much different than college, when she was bouncing majors and struggling to think of a long-term path. She had no focus, whereas he…he'd had a sole focus. Two really. But only one had panned out, he thought, frowning a bit at Abby.

"I'm a chef. Well, a cook," she added quickly. She rearranged her silverware on the counter.

"Here in town?" he frowned, trying to make sense of this. Since when did Abby like to cook? In college she was a fan of cereal for three meals a day if the cafeteria wasn't serving something she liked. But then, he supposed that wasn't fair to assume she was still this way. Years had passed, and he couldn't exactly say he knew her anymore. Much as that hurt.

She gave him an appraising look, as if trying to decide whether or not to elaborate. "At my sister's inn."

In other words, at the Harper House Inn. Well…crap.

His words flooded back to him as quickly as he'd pounded them onto his keyboard and handed them off to his editor, still reeling from the way his reunion with Abby had not gone as he'd hoped it would. *Overly ambitious and limited offerings in a quaint, cottage setting.*

His mouth went dry and he reached for his water glass.

"So when I saw you yesterday…"

"I was working," she finished. She pulled in a breath and released it slowly, and he knew without having to ask what she was thinking about. The review. The review he'd written.

"You should have mentioned it!" he said tightly. She should have. She really, really should have.

"Well…it was certainly no coincidence that I was there," she said. Her gaze was cool and steady.

Zach shifted under the insinuation. "I had no idea you

worked there. I can promise you, I didn't seek you out."

Ah, nice.

"My last name is Harper. You came to eat at the Harper House Inn." She raised an eyebrow. "Obviously, you know I grew up in that house."

"And what if I said I was hoping that I might bump into you?" he asked, looking her square in the eye. Would it be so bad, to catch up after all these years, to remember the good times and all that they'd shared?

He saw the flash of surprise that was all too quickly replaced with something suspicious and wary. "I'd ask why you bothered. After all this time."

He shrugged and stared at the identical plates of club sandwiches that were set in front of them by the twitchy waiter. He hovered for a moment and then, without a word, scurried away.

Zach stared at Abby for a long moment. He could have stared at her all day. Her pretty mouth and bright eyes and the slight upturn of her nose, especially when she was feeling defensive and gave it an extra lift. No girl had ever compared to her. "Would it be so strange to say that I missed you?"

"More like unbelievable," Abby shot back, plucking the frilly toothpick from one of her sandwich triangles and taking a hearty bite.

He watched her chew, wondering how she could possibly be mad at him, still, after all these years. "As memory serves me, you were the one who chose to come back to Oyster Bay," he pointed out, deciding fair was fair here.

Her eyes sprang open. "And you were the one who decided not to."

"Abby." He sighed. Here it was, seven years later, and they were having the exact same argument, no closer now to an understanding than they were back then. "You know I had my work." An opportunity of a lifetime was more like it. A summer internship at the news desk of the biggest broadcasting company in the country. A chance to break in from the ground up and really make something of himself. And he had. Until it all fell apart.

"Ah, yes, your work." She rolled her eyes and took another bite of the sandwich. "And if your work is so important to you, then why are you back now? Why aren't you off interviewing the president of some war-torn country or standing at ground zero of the latest world crisis?"

He stared at his sandwich, knowing he had no appetite for it. "Long story."

"Longer than our story?" she asked. She shook her head. Jabbed a French fry in a pool of ketchup. Set it down. "Forget it," she mumbled under her breath.

"I can see you're still mad at me," he said calmly, even though he didn't feel so calm anymore. He felt angry and defensive and the need to explain his side of things a bit here.

"Damn straight I'm still mad at you!" she all but shouted, garnering a look from the young waiter, who then promptly disappeared through the kitchen door.

Time to diffuse the situation. Time to bring her back to a time and place the he still thought of…probably way too often.

"As mad as that time we had tickets to see that comedian you liked and I drove us to the wrong venue and we missed the first half of the show?"

"Stop," she said, but he could see that she was fighting a smile.

"I thought I was treating you to something really classy, and instead of being at one of the nice theatres downtown, it was way out near the highway, in some semi-abandoned building, and everyone had to be frisked on the way in the door."

"There was no heat and I had to sit there with my gloves on my hands, and my scarf wrapped so tight that I could still see my breath."

"And we were in the last row of the final balcony, and the guy looked more like a grain of sand than a human." Yeah, so much for a holiday treat that year. She was laughing now, and so was he. And it felt good. Too good maybe.

"See?" he said, giving her a little jab with his elbow. It was the first physical contact they'd made since the last time he'd seen her, when she turned and walked away, her auburn hair bouncing at her shoulders, her pace so quick he wasn't sure he could catch up with her even if he'd wanted to. And oh…how he'd wanted to. "We can still laugh together. That's something, isn't it?"

She sighed, a sad sigh. "Yes," she finally admitted. "I suppose it is something."

Something he'd hold onto, he thought. And something that was a whole lot better than nothing.

*

Abby kept her eyes fixed on her plate, because she knew if she looked over at him, which she did every once in a while, it would undo her. From the moment their relationship ended, she had stripped Zach from her life. Gone were the photos, the mementos. Gone were the memories.

She hadn't thought about that night they'd gone to the theatre in a long time. Hadn't allowed herself. But now, it was there, fresh in her mind, as vivid as if it were yesterday. And she was smiling, damn it.

She wasn't supposed to smile when she thought of Zach.

She supposed she could fulfill her curiosity, ask why he was back, what he was doing with his life, what happened to his fancy job. But that would mean she cared. And she couldn't care. Even if a part of her did.

"Well, I should get going," she said, reaching for her wallet, keeping her gaze low. He was too handsome, too…everything.

Everything she'd always wanted. Everything she'd once had.

"Let me," he said. He held up a hand when she began

to protest. "Please. It's the least I can do."

Yes, she supposed it was the least he could do. Besides, contrary to what he may think, she really wasn't in the mood to argue. "Thank you then," she said, tucking her wallet back into her bag.

"Busy plans for the rest of the day?" he asked as they walked outside.

She frowned, not certain where he was going with that question, or if he was just being conversational. "I have some shopping to do," she said. Bridget was low on flour and some of her favorite spices, like nutmeg and ginger. A trip to the market would keep her busy and her mind hopefully off matters—and people—she wished to avoid thinking about.

"You don't have to go back to work?" he said.

"No." Her stomach hurt just thinking about work. "I only work mornings. But who knows how much longer that will last." She kicked at a stone on the sidewalk with the toe of her ballet flat.

"Ah, so see, you haven't changed all that much." Zach grinned, seeming oddly satisfied by this, and crammed his hands into his pockets. "Face it. You have a wandering spirit, just like me."

She knew it was true, or it had been true, that she did have a wandering spirit—once. "I'll have you know that I love my job. I take it seriously, and I'm committed to making it last." She gave him a long, hard look, wondering if he took any greater meaning away from the latter part of her statement.

But he just shrugged and said, "Then why won't it last?"

She huffed out a sigh, wishing she had ridden her bike into town even though that would have been impossible with the basket of scones. Besides, she only lived down the street and around the corner... It suddenly felt like a very far walk.

He was too close. Too handsome. Too present. And her mind was spinning with thoughts that shouldn't be there, of times gone by and dreams that hadn't come true. And hurt. So much hurt.

"It won't last," she started, and then stopped herself. "It *will* last," she said instead. "It will. I just have to make sure of it." Desperate to get off topic, and angry at herself for showing the slightest hint of vulnerability in front of Zach of all people, the person who had hurt her the most, she reached the corner and motioned with her head. "I should get going."

"Maybe I'll bump into you again sometime," he said, daring to give her a grin. Once, that kind of grin would have made her go all weak in the knees and cause her stomach to flutter and all that other nonsense. But not anymore. Well, not too much, at least.

She set a hand to her stomach. Indigestion, she told herself firmly. Stress could do that, and it was turning into a hell of a day.

"It's a small town, so I suppose that's inevitable."

"Well, maybe I'll bump into you," he pressed. "And

maybe next time we'll have two good laughs, not just one."

God, he was impossible.

"I wouldn't count on it," she said, turning to go.

"We used to have a lot of laughs," he said, forcing her to turn around. Her heart began to speed up as their eyes locked. He looked sad, lost almost, not amused as he had only a few moments ago. "I missed those laughs, Abby. I missed you."

The air felt like it was sucked out of her. He missed her. He *missed* her. All those years that she had tried to move on, tried to keep pushing forward, instead of looking back, and it was all coming undone with that one simple sentence. He'd missed her.

But no. No. She hadn't allowed herself to miss him. And she sure as hell wouldn't start now.

"I should go," she said, turning for good this time. She put one foot in front of the other, her stride purposeful. She walked all the way to the end of the block in the direction of her apartment before she remembered she had planned to go to the market. Hesitantly, she turned around, relieved to see he wasn't still standing there, and retraced her steps back toward Main Street.

Her eyes darted through the crowds as she turned onto the busy stretch. Even though it was Monday, there were more people on the streets than there were in the cooler months. People rented houses for the summer, mothers stayed during the week with children while husbands went back to offices in Boston or Portland. Zach was up ahead, crossing the street, and even though she knew she should resist, that she really, really shouldn't care, curiosity finally got the better of her. She stopped at a flower stand, pretending to admire the long peony stems, bringing one to her nose to inhale the sweet fragrance as her eyes followed Zach's steps. Across the street, south on Main, and…into the office of the *Oyster Bay Gazette*.

Wait. What?

With knowing dread, she watched the door, waiting to see if he had just popped in, if he would step right back out, if maybe he'd just gone in to…She didn't know. Buy a paper? Ask Sarah out on a date? But the seconds ticked by with the pounding of her heart, and she knew that he wasn't going to come out. Not anytime soon at least.

Zach Dillon had eaten at the Harper House Inn. And he had been served a burnt scone. And now, now he was behind the glass door of the *Oyster Bay Gazette*.

And despite the fact that he was the award-winning journalist who had covered wars in the Middle East and UN summits, she was the one would be investigating this story further.

Oh yes, she most certainly would.

Abby set the flower back in the bucket, hitched her handbag on her shoulder, and marched all the way to the market, her feet slapping the pavement with fresh determination. So Zach wanted to bump into her again, did he?

Well, next time, she'd be ready.

Chapter Four

On Friday night, the sisters made plans to take Mimi to The Lantern to celebrate her engagement and, Abby knew, for Bridget to get a better idea of the details. Emma was with Ryan for the night, at a father daughter camp dance, and Bridget was picking up both Margo and Mimi on her way into town. Abby decided to arrive early, not because she needed to scout out a good table, but because she hoped to steal a few minutes with her Uncle Chip before everyone arrived and the moment was lost.

She walked into the beachfront restaurant, immediately dismayed to see that the place with packed. Whereas during the fall and winter months she could stop in at most hours of the day and expect Chip to pour her a coffee and lend an ear, tonight he was behind the bar, where he liked to be on busy nights like this, claiming there was no sense in running a restaurant if you didn't get the perk of engaging with the customers.

She envied his confidence when he made statements like this. At the inn, whenever anyone asked to speak to the "chef," she usually entered the dining room on shaking legs. Serenity Hills was a safer audience, even though half the people there were missing teeth or didn't remember their own names. Her courage had come with the Fall Fest pie baking contest that she'd entered. Even though she hadn't won, runner-up had given her the boost she'd needed, and enough nerve to help Bridget with a catering crisis at the inn's first wedding and broach the topic of serving breakfast daily. She'd finally started to find her groove…and then…Well, the review.

The bar was filled with rowdy tourists, in for the weekend, and Abby felt her heart sink as she squeezed into a spot at the end. Her spirits lifted when Chip caught her eye and gave her a wink.

"You here with the group?" he asked, knowing that at least once a week the girls tried to take Mimi to eat at her favorite establishment in town, though lately, that had turned to every other week, and sometimes just once a month.

They were busy. Bridget was balancing the demands from the inn with motherhood and time for her new relationship, and Margo was settling into married life again. Abby would have happily come for dinner with her sisters twice, even three times a week, but they were busy, and…well, that's just how it always was. Maybe she'd start treating Mimi to dinner—just the two of them, the way it used to be before Serenity Hills.

Until Mimi got married, that was. Then Mimi would be accompanied by Earl. The cat kidnapper.

It was one loss after another. When Mimi was still in the house and more capable of not only caring for herself but for Abby, she'd been the one who had gotten Abby through the saddest days of her life. It was Mimi who would coax her into the kitchen, Mimi who would help her find some peace and distraction through recipes and cookbooks and the stories she would tell while they worked side by side, keeping Abby's parents alive through memories. Abby had cherished those days. Maybe it was why she cherished her job at the inn again. That kitchen was her special place.

Her face must have registered all these thoughts, because Chip lifted his chin over the din of the bar, called out to one of his staff to cover him for a few minutes, and then motioned for Abby to follow him into the kitchen.

"Thanks for giving me an excuse to take a break," he said, grinning back at her over his shoulder. "I always forget how crazy the summers are around here. But then, I suppose you're seeing an uptick in business at the inn too."

"Oh yeah." Abby side skirted one of the cooks and wrinkled her nose at the smell of fish as they walked into her uncle's cluttered office, which was barely more than a closet, really. She knew that if she asked, Chip would give her a job in a heartbeat, but working in the kitchen here, as one of the line cooks, and cooking fish all day…it wasn't what she wanted. It wasn't what she dreamed. It would be just a job. Whereas working at the inn…

She swallowed hard. "I don't know if you saw the review in Monday's paper."

Chip sat on the corner of his desk and sighed. "Bridget down about it?"

"Not especially," Abby admitted, hoping that was the truth and not just the stiff upper lip that her eldest sister was known for. Since Monday, Bridget hadn't brought it up again, and so as to not draw attention to her part in it, Abby had never mentioned her stop at the *Oyster Bay Gazette*. Bridget would never have approved. In fact, she'd probably be more than a little horrified.

"Bad reviews happen," Chip said, brushing a hand through the air. "You can't win 'em all."

"Yes, but…" She wanted to say that Chip owned this place, whereas she merely worked for Bridget. She chewed her bottom lip, wondering where to begin. "The inn is new, and Bridget has put so much into it."

"And business is still steady, I assume?"

He knew he had her there. "Yes," she said, with a small smile. The inn was filled up this weekend again, and everyone had checked in by four, as expected.

"No cancellations?"

She shook her head. "No."

"Abby, that review was posted in the *Oyster Bay Gazette*.

No one but the locals read that paper, and besides, it's already Friday. It's yesterday's news."

"It's on the Internet," she pointed out. But that wasn't the worst part. No, her biggest fear was that it was just the first of more bad reviews to come. "You know Bridget," she said carefully. She looked at Chip, gauging how deep she could go here. Chip was close to Bridget, but he was close to all of them, treating them as he did his own two daughters, especially since their parents had passed away.

"I know that Bridget loves you, Abby," he insisted. "She's very impressed with what you're doing at the inn."

"She is?" Abby stared at her uncle in disbelief, wanting so badly to believe this was true. Had she said something? She had the burning urge to ask, but it was immediately replaced by the shame of failing to live up to that unexpected praise. "But see? This is where I'm afraid to let her down."

"You want to know what I think about that?" He cocked an eyebrow, and something told Abby that whether she wanted to know the answer or not, he was going to tell her. "Stop being afraid."

She gave a wan smile. Easier said than done somehow. "Thanks, Chip."

"Hey, it's why you girls all come to see me." He grinned, and Abby reached over to give him a hug. "Now, if you could do me a favor and tell *my* girls how wise I am next time you see them, I'd appreciate it. Not that Hannah ever visits."

"It's different with your own parents," Abby reassured him, but even as she said it, something tugged in her chest and Chip's blue eyes went a little flat. Abby knew he missed his sister every bit as much as she missed her mother.

"I'm always here for you, Abby," he said. He cleared his throat as he pushed himself off his desk.

"I know," she said, feeling a little better, just as she knew she would. Chip was one of the reasons she could never leave this town. One of the reasons she'd come back. You might make friends in other places, but family…family couldn't be taken for granted. She'd learned that the hard way.

By the time they'd made it back to the dining room, her sisters and grandmother were walking through the door, and Chip led them over to one of the best tables with a view of the harbor. Mimi was dressed in her favorite pink pant suit, and she'd even added matching lipstick tonight. Bridget set her phone on the table, in case Ryan called about Emma, and Margo ordered a bottle of wine and four glasses, eliminating the need for anyone to ask if she was pregnant yet.

"A toast," Margo said, holding up her glass of Chardonnay when a bottle had been corked and poured. "To Mimi."

"To Mimi," they all said, clinking glasses.

"And Earl!" Bridget added. "I have to say, Mimi, that

his courtship tactics will not be forgotten." The girls exchanged glances, and Abby sipped her drink to hide her smile.

"Just think, a second wedding this year already," Margo marveled, looking down at her own ring. She glanced at Bridget. "Three is a charm, you know."

Three meaning Bridget, not Abby, of course. Nope, Abby wasn't the settling down type in their opinions, and while she knew that she was responsible for fostering that image, it didn't sit well that they so easily accepted it. Once there was a time when she would have loved nothing more than to settle down, after all.

Bridget blushed and tucked a loose strand of hair behind her ears. "We'll see. Jack and I are taking it slow." She shrugged, but Abby knew she was just being modest. Jack had moved to Oyster Bay to be near her. There was no doubt in anyone's mind that wedding bells would soon be heard.

"That just leaves you, Abby," Mimi remarked, but not to Abby's relief. "Still have your eye on that nurse, or are you back together with that young homeless man?"

Abby's cheeks heated. "Chase was not homeless," she said defensively, wondering why she was bothering to stick up for a guy who had run off with his band, never to be heard from again. Sure, it had been disappointing, and she had dared to think she might really enjoy his company. And she did. For a while. But who was she kidding? The man lived in a van and dumpster dove for his supper. He wasn't a long-term option. And maybe…maybe that's what had been appealing.

"You really know how to pick 'em," Margo said, laughing. Then, being the peacemaker that she was, she set a hand on Abby's wrist. "You're such a fun, sweet girl, Abby. Don't sell yourself short."

Was that what she was doing? Selling herself short? She reached for her wine glass and took another long sip. Looking back at the various men she'd dated since Zach, she could almost venture to say she'd done just that. It was easier that way. Easier to be with someone casual and fun, easier to know that at the end of the day, despite physical attraction, there was no future, and no risk of really wanting one.

"You're forgetting she did date Zach Dillon at one point," Bridget said, rising to her defense.

At the mere mention of his name, Abby considered excusing herself to the bathroom. But it was too late. Margo was mentioning that he was seen at the inn on Sunday and now everyone was discussing his jet-setting lifestyle and pondering what might have brought him back to town.

"His parents are in fine health," Bridget said, opening her menu. "I saw his mother at the library last month. His dad just retired and I heard he plays tennis every morning."

Margo turned to Abby, as if she might be able to shed more light on the situation. Abby just shrugged and again reached for her wine glass, until she saw Mimi's brow pinch across the table, and she reached for her water instead. "Beats me. We lost touch after college."

That seemed to satisfy the table; after all, it wasn't uncharacteristic for her, was it? While they'd all stuck with one person and then, when that ended, stuck to the next, Abby had bounced around. From job to job. Guy to guy.

But they didn't understand, didn't get it. You couldn't stick to someone who didn't want to stick to you. And Zach hadn't. He'd only stuck with one thing. His job.

Until now, she thought, wondering again just what could have been important enough to have brought him back to town.

*

Zach's phone buzzed on the coffee table. He didn't bother looking at the screen. It would likely be his mother, asking again if he wanted to come to dinner tonight, and he hated to continue to let her down. She was worried, he knew. Wondering why he'd come back to town so suddenly. Why he was sleeping on his sister's couch instead of moving into his childhood bedroom. Why he wouldn't talk about his life, his job, or everything he'd left behind.

But how did you explain it? His mother had been born and raised in Oyster Bay, Maine. Population so small that he could probably name half the residents of the town off his head. Her days were full of walks to the beach, walks into town, with its quaint boutiques and restaurants.

Sunday mornings were spent at church followed by volunteer afternoons at the community center, where she chaired the various festivals the town was known for: the Flower Fest, Fall Fest, and the annual Christmas bazaar. Her life was simple and reliable and far from spontaneous. All things that used to bore him; things he couldn't wait to run from.

Things he now appreciated more than ever.

"Mom again?" His sister, Melanie, barely looked up from the television screen. It was her usual evening routine: she recorded her favorite soap operas during the day and watched them at night when she returned from her job at Bayside Brides. Shows that used to play in their childhood home when they were kids and now, years after he'd been away, the same characters' lives unfolded on the screen, much the way they did here in sleepy Oyster Bay.

Zach shoved the phone in his pocket, ignoring the flashing blue light in the corner. He'd call his parents tomorrow, tell them he'd been out with friends tonight. Maybe it would even be the truth. Maybe he'd run into some of his old buddies from high school, have a beer, escape for a bit.

"They bug you as much as they bug me?" he asked Melanie, who was perfectly content in her armchair and flannel pajamas at seven sharp each night, regardless of the summer heat. Zach secretly found this worrisome. Melanie had always been a studious girl, but a pretty one, too. Now, in her late twenties, he was alarmed to see that she was all too content to shed her work clothes within minutes of walking through the door, clearly deciding she was in for the night. Her face was washed of makeup, and contact lenses were replaced with unforgiving glasses. Shouldn't she be…dating? Going out with friends? Oyster Bay's social scene wasn't exactly thriving, but surely it was a little more exciting than television at times?

"They've had me around for years," Melanie said as she reached for a bag of pretzels, her preferred evening snack. "You're a novelty."

Lucky him. He'd come back to Oyster Bay to hide, not to share, and he was grateful that Melanie at least hadn't pressed very much. All she asked from him was that he was done showering by seven each morning and that he didn't use all the hot water.

"Why don't we go out tonight?" he suddenly suggested, not sure if he was doing it for her sake or his own. He was starting to feel restless again, starting to get that weird sensation in his gut that told him he needed a distraction and fast.

"Out?" She looked at him in something close to horror. "I haven't finished today's episode, and Friday is always a cliffhanger, you know that."

Yes, he did, just like he knew that Miranda and Yvette had each married and divorced the same man eight times each since he was ten years old and they were still squabbling over it on today's episode, more than two decades later.

"Well, I'll be back in a bit. Call me if you change your mind," he said, but she wouldn't, he knew, and that made him sad, almost as sad as he felt for himself at times. Eventually he'd have to talk with her, be the big brother he was and have a heart to heart and see what was going on. But not tonight. Tonight Melanie wanted to watch her favorite show. Small pleasures. Who was he to stop her?

Melanie's apartment was two blocks off Main, walking distance to the bridal shop she co-owned with their cousin Chloe, and he was in the heart of town within minutes. The sidewalks were busy, and the sun was low on the horizon, casting a warm glow over the oceanfront, visible at each intersection, where the buildings parted and the sky opened up.

There was Dunley's, owned by Ryan Dunley, who used to be married to Bridget, but the crowds were big, too big, and he needed someplace a little more laidback. The Lantern was up ahead. A classic seaside joint with nautical decorations and big burgers and a bar that always showed the game.

And it happened to be owned by Abby's uncle. Someone she was still in good with. The odds were in his favor.

Decision made, he thought, quickening his pace.

There was a line outside the door, tourists happy to put their names on a reservation list and sit on the weather-worn benches, enjoying the salty breeze and the warm glow of the fading sun on their shoulders. Time moved slower in Oyster Bay. People did, too. He was all too aware in the two weeks since he'd returned that he walked faster, ate faster, talked faster than everyone else. He needed to calm down, relax, but that was easier said than done. His body might be here in this quiet community, but his mind was still running, jumping from topic to topic, still fighting the images that seemed burned in his brain of another time and another place. Another world, really.

He opened the door and pushed through the crowds of people—young couples holding hands, up from the city for a romantic weekend—and families with tired-looking kids, whining they were hungry—and saddled up to the bar. There was one open seat at the corner and he kept his eye on it, hurrying again, this time to reach something, something tangible, not something he couldn't identify.

He sighed into a smile as he sat down, feeling the small victory.

"Zachary Dillon!" Chip Donovan grinned from the end of the bar. "That's a face I haven't seen in a long time."

Zach felt the strange mix of guilt and nostalgia that plagued him everywhere he went since coming back to town. While he'd been away, his life changing from week to week, life here had remained the same. Chip still ran The Lantern. His parents still lived in this yellow Cape.

Abby still hated him.

He swallowed hard on that thought. "It's been a while," he admitted.

"What can I get for you?"

"Whatever's on tap," he said. "And a lobster roll." No matter where he went or how far he traveled, nothing could top the lobster rolls you could get in Oyster Bay.

"Have you seen Abby yet?" Chip asked, as he slid his beer against the bar.

Zach took a long sip before answering. "Around town."

"Well, I'm sure she'd be happy to see you," Chip said, and Zach almost choked on his beer. It took everything in him not to set the guy straight. He'd chosen his path; Abby had chosen hers. And somehow he was the bad guy in this equation.

"Something tells me I'm not exactly her favorite person at the moment," he said mildly.

Chip just gave him a slow grin and said, "Don't look now, but she's sitting at the back of the room with her sisters, and last time I checked, women don't smooth their hair when they don't care…"

Zach grinned slowly and took another sip of his beer. It was cold and frothy and went down easily. So Abby was sitting behind him, was she?

Looked like they had another chance to run into each other then. And who knew…maybe three times was the charm.

*

Abby could barely concentrate on the conversation going on around her. Mimi was talking about Pudgie, something about him being part of the wedding, and Margo was protesting, loudly.

"You cannot have a cat be part of your wedding," she insisted, her face growing red.

"It's my wedding day and I'll do as I see fit," Mimi snipped. "Besides, Pudgie would be the perfect ring bearer." Her eyes turned wistful as if she were imagining the day. "They make these sweet little bow tie collars. Pudgie will look positively dapper."

"Well, there is still time to sort out the details," Bridget said, giving Margo a warning look. "Mid-July is certainly a hot time of year for an outdoor wedding."

"Pudgie likes the outdoors. Besides, I want to be married surrounded by fresh air and flowers."

They shifted topics to something safer. The cake, and which flavor would be best. Abby's eyes kept darting to the bar, where Zach was sitting, back to her, his eyes on the baseball game being shown on one of the screens. Every now and again Chip would say something and burst out laughing. Abby's eyes narrowed. The traitor!

Not that he knew, in fairness, just how deep her feelings had gone. To them, Zach was just one of many, not the one.

The one. She didn't have the one. The one implied the one you ended up with. The one you married. The one that was meant to be.

No. Zach didn't fit that description. He'd never been the one. Even if, for a while, it seemed that he would be.

"Abby?"

She jumped in her seat, realizing that all three women were now staring at her, and possibly had been for some time.

"What?" she asked. Her face was on fire, and she reached for a water glass, only to find it was empty.

"You haven't been paying attention to anything we've said!" Bridget accused.

"Yes, I have." Abby lifted her chin indignantly.

"Then tell us what flavor cake Mimi wants you to bake for her wedding."

God, Bridget could be insufferable when she got like this, but it was just how she'd always been, oldest of the three, surrogate mother when their own was taken far too soon.

"Well that would obviously be—" Abby blinked. "Wait. Did you just say you want *me* to bake the cake, Mimi?" A huge smile broke out over her face and all at once a dozen pictures popped into her head of three-tiered white confections.

"That's right. The theme is cats. I want a chocolate cake shaped like a cat head. Mind you don't forget the whiskers."

Abby's mouth drew into a straight line as she eyed her sisters. Was this some sort of gag because she hadn't been paying attention?

Margo seemed to be blinking back tears of either

despair or frustration and Bridget said again, "There is still plenty of time to sort out the details." Turning to Abby, she said with a secret smile, "And what's had you so distracted tonight? You've barely touched your pasta, and I notice that Zach Dillon is up at the bar chatting with Chip."

"So?" But as soon as she saw the sparkle in Bridget's clear blue eyes, Abby knew she'd given herself away.

"So you noticed," Bridget grinned. "Think there's still any spark left?"

"No," Abby said firmly.

"Have your eye on someone else then?" Bridget asked.

Abby knew it wasn't in malice, but something about the way her sister said it stung. Was this really the way they thought of her? The impression she gave off? She could set them straight here and now, but what good was there in telling them that at one point in time she had been in love? Really, maybe she never was. How could you be in love with someone who didn't return the favor in the end?

"Right now, all I care about is my job," she said firmly, and that was the truth.

She didn't care about Zach. Or the fact that he was in the room. And that the bathroom didn't have a window she could crawl out of, at least not without getting wedged in it.

Chapter Five

Abby kept one eye trained on Zach as her sisters stood and Bridget helped Mimi out of the chair. Though they'd come separately, and the assumption was that Abby would walk home and Bridget would drop Margo off and then return Mimi to Serenity Hills before going back to the inn, Abby hesitated as they made their way to the door.

She had a decision to make, and quick. She could leave, pretend she hadn't seen Zach or that she didn't care—which she didn't, of course. Or she could walk over to him, say hello all casually and calmly, show her sisters that there was nothing to talk about and prove to herself that it didn't hurt to look into those clear blue eyes anymore.

The decision was made for her when Chip, a big grin

plastered on his face, called out, "Hey, Abby! Look who's back in town!"

Her lids fluttered with forced patience. Well, fabulous.

Margo could barely hide her smile and Bridget all but pushed her toward the bar. "You go ahead and stay."

"I'm tired," she growled in return.

Bridget's eyebrows rose. "Nonsense! You're young and single and it's not even eight on a Friday night!"

My, how was this for irony? Not so long ago it was Abby who was encouraging Bridget to get out, stay out, flirt a little. And now, it was her turn.

The bar was full. Some faces she recognized, others, of tourists, she didn't. But the only one she saw was Zach's, looking over his shoulder at her, his expression a little sheepish.

Aw, damn it. She wasn't going to be painted as the bad guy in this picture. Uh-uh. No way. Zach had made his decision fair and square, and he wasn't allowed to suddenly be the victim, not when he probably hadn't spared her a thought since the day she'd boarded the bus back to Oyster Bay.

I missed you.

The words echoed in her mind. Tugged at her heart.

She swallowed hard, looking back at her sisters' expectant faces, at Bridget, who had given her so much and was really only hoping for the best for her in this moment. It was only one drink, she told herself. And maybe, just maybe, she'd get to the root of who wrote that review.

With that in mind, she bid her now giddy sisters goodnight, squared her shoulders, and, really wishing that she had done something more interesting with her hair than just barely run a brush through it, walked straight over to Zach.

And yes, her legs were shaking. Not that she'd let him know that.

*

Zach eyed Abby warily. She was beelining toward him, but she wasn't smiling. Still, she wasn't scowling either.

He grinned, but she didn't return the gesture.

"Hey." He made a motion of scooting over to the next stool, leaving the nearest space for her. With what he would call extreme hesitation, she sat down. So this was how it was going to be then.

"Can I get you something to drink?" he asked, by way of a more formal greeting. She shook her head, but he caught the eye of the closest bartender anyway. "A glass of white wine for my friend, please." Friend. He didn't know what other word to use. Once she had been his *girlfriend*. Now she was just a *friend*. Even though, all things considered, they were hardly even that.

"You remembered," she said, seeming surprised.

"Of course I remembered. It wasn't that long ago." The last half of their nearly four-year relationship, they would spend every Saturday night at a little wine bar around the corner from his grad school apartment (a big step up from the dorms of undergrad that she was still living in, even if it was a little box of a place that could barely even be called a studio, but which had four walls and a door and all the personal items that mattered to him at the time). Abby ordered a white wine spritzer at first, eventually moving on to the real thing when she'd gotten used to the taste of it. It was a small place, with stone walls and dim lighting and a single motive candle in the center of the table that didn't always last the night. It was their place. And when things ended between them, he never returned. Now he had a sudden longing to go back, to sit in that bar, to turn back time.

"Seven years is pretty long ago to me," she replied.

It felt like seven months and seven hundred all at once. So much had happened in those years, so many experiences, some exciting, some scary, some…better forgotten. But what had Abby done in those seven years? Had she met someone? Loved someone?

"Remember that little wine bar…" he grinned at her, but she just stared at him flatly. "Come on. Our place. They always played that French café music you liked. And they had those long, red velvet curtains." Surely she remembered!

"That was a long time ago," was all she said, looking away.

He turned to his beer. She was making this harder than it needed to be. "So you became a cook in those seven years." He didn't want to dwell on this topic. Not with the guilt of that review still stirring in his gut, making him uneasy. "Anything else?"

Her eyes flashed on him. "Just because I didn't jet set around the world for the better part of a decade doesn't mean I was sitting here skipping stones all that time."

He blinked, surprised at the anger in her tone. She really hated him. And that...crushed him. "Okay, then, tell me. Tell me everything."

He longed to hear it. To know what she'd done with her life. To know that she'd been okay. The bits of information he'd gotten from his mother had been like gold, rare and special, and something to treasure. He didn't allow himself to ask too much, knowing there was no point, but he discovered enough...enough to know that she was okay, and maybe even happy.

She studied him for a long time. Long enough for her drink to arrive. Finally she let out a long sigh. "Are you following me?"

Well, damn. "Now why would I do that?"

"Hmm, let's see...first you show up at the inn. At my childhood home, mind you. Then I see you at Jojo's. Now here."

He shrugged and reached for his second beer of the night. "This place is popular. It was this or Dunley's."

"Also a family place," she reminded him. "Since Bridget's divorce, I don't go in there as much."

"And Margo is back in town?" he asked.

She nodded. "Margo is also divorced, though. Well, remarried actually. To Eddie Boyd?"

My, a lot had happened in those seven years, to the Harper family, at least. "Eddie Boyd? They dated in high school."

Abby sipped her drink and nodded. "Yep. Well, he's the town sheriff now and Margo's an interior designer, but you probably knew that part already."

He did. Margo was two years ahead of him in school, and Abby was two behind, and for as long he could remember living in Oyster Bay, he'd never even noticed Abby. They didn't hang out in the same circles and she was just a little kid back in grade school, but when she'd come to Boston for college everything had changed.

"And Bridget owns the inn..." he was eager to keep the conversation going, like this, casual, almost as if they were getting to know each other all over again.

"Yep. She's dating someone now. Sure took her long enough." Abby seemed to roll her eyes at no one in particular. "And he moved to town recently. I imagine they'll get married soon." She sighed.

"And you like working for her at the inn?" Last he knew, Abby had a strained relationship with Bridget. It wasn't terrible, more like Abby wanted to be close to her sister and Bridget wanted to play mother hen. Especially after their parents had died.

Zach picked up his drink again, drank it dry. He still felt shame when he thought back to that time, the circumstances that had led to them breaking up and going their separate ways. He'd convinced himself at the time that he was doing what was best for both of them, that it was the right thing, the only thing. But now he wasn't so sure of anything anymore.

Other than the fact that now, seeing Abby again, he had missed her. And he didn't want to miss her again.

"I love working at the inn," Abby said firmly. She skirted a glance at him. "But I'm not so sure my sister will keep me on. It's been a trial period, of sorts." Her voice was shaky, but all too soon, her eyes narrowed.

"Someone," she said, giving him a pointed stare that did the intended job of making him sweat a little, "wrote a bad review of the inn. Specifically, they wrote a bad review of my food."

He blinked at her, wondering if she knew, if he'd been exposed as the reporter, or if she was feeling him out, calling his bluff.

It was the latter, he decided. If Abby knew for certain that he had written that stupid article, then she would have raised hell by now.

"Oh now, are you referring to that article from Monday's paper?" he asked, careful to neither admit nor deny his part in it.

Her eyes sparked. "I am."

He frowned, trying to recall the words, the exact description. Yes, the scones had been burned, something that really couldn't be overlooked. But he'd been sure to mention the casual yet elegant ambience, the personal touches that could only be found at an inn as opposed to a restaurant in town...

Who was he kidding? He wasn't cut out for the job. He'd only taken the assignment because he was the new guy and because Will Zimmerman, who was supposed to be filling that slot, came down with a cold. And who got colds in the summertime, anyway? He blamed it on his kids. Claimed that they were always coming home with germs. From school, from camp, from everywhere.

Zach hadn't really believed him until, sure enough, Will came back to work on Wednesday, sniffling and sneezing and carrying a bottle of hand sanitizer that smelled like rubbing alcohol.

He remembered Will from school. He remembered everyone in town from back in school. Will had been captain of the lacrosse team and head of the student council. Now Will took time off of work for a cold. When Zach considered what he used to do get a good story, the lengths he would take to secure a hot interview…it made him question his decision to return to Oyster Bay. It made him question a lot of things, like what would he do if he didn't stay in Oyster Bay? Get a desk job at a big paper in New York?

His stomach started to turn every time he considered his options, none of which seemed ideal.

Abby, he realized, was watching him. Closely. He pulled himself back to the present, his gaze roaming her face, drifting down to her mouth and back up to her stone-cold eyes.

"Oh now, that article wasn't so bad, from what I

recall." It had been balanced. And honest. Objective. He'd just been trying to do his job, removing any personal connection he had to the Harper family.

"Well, it was bad enough," she said, holding his gaze. "Bad enough to possibly put a new small business in trouble!"

"There are only two hotels in this town and your sister owns one of them," he pointed out. Most people rented cottages for the summer, even though they went for a pretty price. He'd been surprised to see how much a monthly studio cost, but it still wasn't enough to tempt him back to his childhood bedroom. It was bad enough that his mother had stopped by Melanie's apartment last week, insisting she do his laundry, and had folded all his boxers into tight little squares before setting them back in his suitcase, considering Melanie didn't have a spare dresser for him. The pull-out couch wouldn't be a long-term option either. Not that anything was. He'd grown used to the transient life. The mini-bars. The lack of personal artifacts. The ability to pack up and leave as soon as he needed to.

"It doesn't help matters though." She pinched her lips. "If someone has a choice between the Oyster Bay Hotel or the Harper House Inn, this article might be the decision maker."

"They're totally different experiences," he disagreed. "People who like hotels will stay at a hotel. People who don't need as many services will opt for the inn."

He looked at her, seeing by the hurt in her eyes that he

wasn't saying anything to make her feel better. He reached out, set a hand on her wrist, as naturally as he had once done so many times he'd lost count. Her skin was cool to the touch, and soft, and her eyes flashed with alarm, or maybe even warning. But he didn't care. He left it there. It felt good. It felt…right.

And seldom else felt right just now.

*

Abby pulled her arm from the counter and shoved it onto her lap, out of reach. She regretted not wearing something more modest, like a cardigan or a turtleneck, even if it was June and the breeze off the bay did little to offset the heat most days.

"So…staying with your parents?" Why was she even asking? And where was her drink?

"With Melanie," he said.

Ah, Melanie. Poor girl could probably use the company right now, considering how Doug McKinney had ceremoniously dumped her on Valentine's Day. Melanie had been expecting a bouquet of roses and a box of chocolates and instead she got a phone call telling her that Doug felt they should see other people.

Abby knew all this because Melanie's best friend, Leah, worked at Angie's. And Leah talked to Angie, who talked to Bridget, and well…that was Oyster Bay for you. There were no secrets. Not for long, at least.

"She must like having the company," Abby said.

Zach didn't look so sure. "I'm worried about her, actually. She spends all her free time watching television, and she treats the characters on the shows like…"

"Friends?" Abby finished for him.

He looked at her with such relief, such comfort that she understood, that for a moment, Abby forgot that she hated him.

"It's not easy for a single girl in Oyster Bay. Most people moved on or got married by now." She struggled to look at him when she said this. Of course, she fell into the same boat as Melanie, minus the Valentine's Day fiasco, of course. Word around town was that Melanie had given up. Stopped wearing makeup, gained a few pounds, and had turned to boxed wine instead of the bottled stuff.

"And you?" Zach surprised her by saying.

She looked sharply at him. He couldn't be serious.

"And me?" Her heart was starting to race and she didn't even know how to answer this question. What could she say? Oh, I've dated casually for years, trying to convince myself that each guy I meet is wonderful and that I might even be in love, when let's face it, no one ever compared to you?

She'd sooner drink ocean water, and she'd accidentally slurped down enough as a kid to know just how unpleasant that could be.

"Have you…found someone?" His expression was, possibly for the first time, unreadable, and Abby forced herself to look him in the eye, properly, even though it hurt like hell. Those sea blue eyes and thick lashes and that mouth that lifted ever so slightly at the corner.

"Well, I haven't *not* found someone," she said, hating the defensive edge that had crept into her tone. After all, it wasn't like she had sat alone in her pajamas for all these years, watching television and eating chips and drinking boxed wine.

Oh, Melanie, she thought. She'd have invited her out, but seeing that she was Zach's sister and all...Yeah. Too weird.

"Well." Zach seemed to stiffen. He turned away from her, grabbed his beer and took a long sip. His eyes went to the game playing on one of the televisions above the bar. Yankees were up at bat. Zach was a Sox fan. "That's good. That's...great."

He didn't seem to think it was so great and she hated how much this pleased her. She knew she could ask, return the question and continue the conversation, but she'd never been the masochistic type. Of course Zach had dated, maybe he'd even fallen in love. Maybe he was in a relationship now, though given that he was back here shacking up on Melanie's couch, she doubted that.

Oh, another flutter. She pushed it firmly back in place.

"So what brings you back to town?" This she wanted to know.

"Work." He shrugged. Glanced at her and looked back at the game. He was getting uncomfortable and this was very interesting.

"So you said," she said, sipping her wine when it was finally presented to her. God, she would need two more of these to get through another ten minutes beside Zach. He still scrubbed with the same soap. It left that woodsy smell on his skin long after he'd showered and lingered in his clothes, and sometimes even on hers. "Special assignment?"

She was staring at him, waiting for him to flinch, to reveal something that she might pounce on, but he just shrugged and said, "I'm actually between jobs at the moment."

"You left the paper?" After all, he'd only worked for the biggest one in the country, as a lead investigative reporter, nonetheless. Sure, she'd read a few of his articles. For a while.

"It was time for a change," he said tightly. He turned away from her, eyes fixed hard on the game, and she knew she wouldn't get much further with him right now. Zach could be strangely distant when he wanted to be, tight lipped and reserved, while she... she couldn't hold back. No matter how badly she wanted to keep things closer to her chest, her emotions always brewed to the surface and everything burst out of her in one big rush. It was killing her not to just ask, to come flat out and demand to know if he wrote the bad review.

But he had. Of course he had. And knowing he did and changing that outcome were two very different things. And this was why, for once, her emotions would not be her guide. For once, she'd be patient, and use her head.

After all, there was no more reason to use her heart when it came to Zach Dillon.

And with that, she stood, smiled sweetly and bid him good night. And she didn't look back as she walked out the door, just like she hadn't looked back seven years ago, much as she longed to.

Chapter Six

Abby stood in the kitchen of the inn, staring at the mound of dough she'd just mixed for some homemade sourdough bread. She dusted her hands in flour and, almost unable to resist, gave the dough a hard punch. Oh, that felt good. So good, in fact, that she did it again, and again, and she didn't stop until she felt the heat of someone's eyes on hers and looked up to see Margo standing in the kitchen doorway, trying not to laugh.

"Maybe you should try a kickboxing class next time," she said, coming into the room.

It was Sunday, the day that Eddie caught up on paperwork and pulled a shift dealing with the typical petty crimes that happened in Oyster Bay: a lost wallet, a missing cat, a fender bender. Margo took the time to help at the inn, and today, more than any other day, Abby was grateful to have her here.

"Sorry, I just feel…agitated." Abby softened her stance on the dough to a rough knead.

"So I can see. Does this have anything to do with a certain ex-boyfriend being back in town after a long absence?" she asked.

Maybe, Abby thought. Probably. And if anyone could understand, it would be Margo. After all, she hadn't been very happy to see Eddie after he returned to town. But then she got used to it. And then…

Well. She punched the dough. No sense in thinking that her story would end like Margo's had. Eddie and Margo had always loved each other. Always wanted the same things, really. And Zach had always wanted something different. He wanted glamour and excitement and all the things that could never be found in sleepy Maine. He wanted adventure. He wanted to change the world.

But he'd wanted her, too. Up until she'd made it clear that she needed to come home. And then…

"It's about the review," she said instead. As much as she would have loved to confide in Margo, it would open up old wounds and allow emotions that shouldn't exist to flow.

"You're still upset about that?" Margo looked amused. "It's yesterday's news, Abby!"

"Not when it's on the Internet forever," Abby said, giving her a knowing look.

Margo sighed and slid onto a barstool. The brunch had ended twenty minutes ago, and the dishes had been cleared along the way. Bridget had just darted out to pick up Emma from Ryan's apartment, and the house was theirs. Or, the kitchen at least. From the other side of the house, Abby could make out the muffled sounds of guests relaxing in the lobby before heading to the beach or town for the day.

"We were booked full today. Does that make you feel any better?"

Abby shaped the bread into a loaf. She was making it as much for herself as she was for Bridget. A gift, and a wonderful way to pound out her emotions as it had turned out.

"I just don't want to give Bridget any reason to second-guess our arrangement, that's all."

Margo frowned. "You're working hard, Abby. Everyone can see that."

"Yes, but Bridget still views me as a child."

"She's oldest. That's her job." Margo shrugged, but Abby didn't agree. It was easy for her to say, being closer in age to Bridget, being Bridget's friend. When Bridget had decided to turn this house into an inn, she'd enlisted Margo to redesign the space, and the two of them had meetings, lots of meetings, meetings that Abby hadn't been a part of, and desperately wanted to be. Margo hadn't needed to beg for a chance to contribute the way Abby had.

"You two are close. Like…equals," she realized. Both

had been married. Both had actual careers. "Bridget and I don't have that. We never did." Sure, there had been times when she turned to Bridget. Times she'd even needed her. But Bridget was busy. She'd had an infant when their parents died, and then there was the divorce…Abby was another responsibility that Bridget couldn't handle. Mimi had taken her in, comforted her, but Abby always felt the longing for her sister. Always hoped for that bond that had never yet come. Oh, Bridget tried, in her own way, of course. She'd tell Abby that she needed to get a stable job. That she needed to figure out her life. She'd try to advise her on things like managing her bank account and planning for her future. But that stuff was boring. And sometimes all Abby hoped for was that Bridget might use the same time she spent lecturing her to just…sit with her. There were the occasional dinners, and the less frequent coffees, and those were…nice. But Bridget was busy. How many times over the years had she heard Bridget talk about everything she had to do? Emma needed to be picked up and shuffled to dance and in between there was grocery shopping and laundry and a job to balance too. It was very clear that Abby couldn't fit into any of that.

Now that Bridget was back in this house, managing the inn, there was a chance for Abby to be close to her. To have more of the connection she'd always wanted.

But not if Bridget viewed her as the little girl who couldn't keep her closet clean, or the young woman who didn't know how to balance a checkbook.

"I thought you two were getting closer." Margo looked perplexed.

"We are, in a way." Abby set the loaf of dough on the baking sheet. There had been a few good laughs recently, like the time that a guest in Room Two had clogged the toilet and checked out early from the embarrassment. "But she's now my boss in addition to my sister. It's tricky."

"And here I thought you were upset about seeing Zach," Margo joked. She paused for a moment, her smile slipping as she met Abby's eye. "How did it go after we left you?"

Abby quickly busied herself with the dough. She'd pounded it so much that it was no doubt over mixed, but the folks at Serenity Hills might not care. They were a forgiving lot. So long as you brought them stuff from the "outside," they loved you.

"Oh, fine, fine." This is where the conversation stopped, Abby decided. "We just had a drink, no biggie."

No biggie? Since when did she say stuff like that? And damn it, but she had the distinct impression that her cheeks were growing hot, and not because the oven had finished preheating.

Margo was giving her a funny look, but said nothing more. "Well," she said, "I'm off. Mimi wants to discuss color schemes for her wedding."

The sisters exchanged a grin. At the end of their meal on Friday night, Mimi was discussing an early July wedding. "Does she really want to wear a silk suit in that heat?" It was nearly as crazy as the idea of a cat-shaped wedding cake, which Abby still couldn't quite come to terms with, but would eventually have to give more thought.

Margo raised her eyebrows as she slid off the chair and slung her handbag over her shoulder. "It would seem so. But you know, Mimi. She's still wearing her wool sweaters in the evenings most days."

Abby laughed. "True." She waved to her sister as she exited out the back door, thinking that Bridget would be back anytime and now she'd only have little Emma to rely on as buffer. Being alone with Bridget was something she'd avoided at all costs since Monday. She could leave. After all, the kitchen was spotless, or would be, once she finished wiping the flour off the island counter, and she'd finished prepping for tomorrow.

She grinned to herself. No use standing around, watching the bread bake, when she could whip up another batch of her truly delectable blueberry scones.

In fact, she knew just the person who might enjoy one with his afternoon coffee...

*

Two hours later, Abby propped her bike against a tree in front of the offices of the *Oyster Bay Gazette* and gently pulled the basket of scones from her bicycle basket, happy to note that the sun had kept them warm.

There was indeed an OPEN sign on the door, and Sarah was behind the desk. She pushed through the door and grinned at Sarah, who was filing her nails. She looked up guiltily, but Abby just brushed a hand through the air. "What else are you going to do between calls?"

"Hardly anyone calls on Sundays. But I could finish filing this paperwork…" she gestured to a large stack that had been pushed to one side of her desk.

"I used to work down the street at the insurance office." And the doctor's office, and the law office, and a few other places, too, not that Abby needed to mention this. She leaned forward and whispered, "I could paint both hands and feet between calls some days."

Sarah laughed, and Abby did too, thinking that it felt like half a lifetime ago, not just a little over a year ago, when she was sitting in that soulless grey office, with only a dying waxy houseplant for a splash of color, reporting to Fred, the sad, middle-aged man who had inherited the business from his father and took it way too seriously, if anyone were to ask her, which they never did.

When she'd given her notice two months into the job, deciding that happiness was more important than a steady paycheck and that she might be more suited to dog walking (which she did before realizing you still had to walk the dogs even when it rained, and then taking a job at a doctor's office for a few months), Fred's jaw had slacked for a full five minutes, and when he'd finally recovered from the shock, he claimed he couldn't understand why she didn't want a future with the company.

Abby had laughed the whole way home over that. A future with an insurance company! Yeah, that had never been in the cards.

But then, neither had trying to sweeten up her ex with scones.

"We should go get a pedicure sometime," she said to Sarah. She'd been so wrapped up in her new job at the inn that summer had snuck up on her, and she was suddenly all too aware that it was sandal season and she wasn't exactly prepared for it.

"I'd love that," Sarah said, brightening, and Abby realized that she was excited for it. It had been a long time since she'd gone out with a girlfriend. Most of her friends from growing up had moved to Portland or Boston, and the few that stayed had settled into married life when she was still going out to dinner with the summer guys. A few even had kids now. They'd tried to keep in touch, promising girls nights and much needed wine, but those get togethers were few and far between and more and more didn't happen at all. And often when they did, they talked about things like babies and kids, and even though Abby tried to chime in about Emma, it wasn't the same, and they knew it.

"Just don't tell your grandmother," Abby chided.

Sarah's eyes went round. "Oh no. At Serenity Hills, we'll pretend we don't even know each other."

"I might even give you the stink eye. Out of loyalty, of

course."

They laughed. Finally, Abby worked up the courage to say what she had come to ask. "So. Any more thoughts about who could have written that review?"

She waited for it, the confirmation, mentally crossing her fingers and toes. It was what she needed, really, just the proof to seal what she already knew. And then.... What? She already knew that Zach was a class-A jerk. He'd proven that to her when he'd put his job before their relationship.

She glanced down the hall, wondering if he was here today. Wondering if she should have worn something a little cuter in case he was.

Oh now, really, Abby. She was here on a mission.

She straightened her basket. It didn't matter if he was a jerk, she reminded herself. What mattered was that he wrote a retraction, or at the very least a glowing review of her scones that could be forever found on the Internet. She might even frame it and hang it in the dining room at the inn. With Bridget's approval, of course...

"No one has said anything," Sarah said slowly, "but I'm listening."

Abby supposed it was all she could expect, and it had been worth a try. "Thanks. Mind sharing these again today?"

"With pleasure!" Sarah said, reaching to help herself to a particularly large scone on top.

Abby couldn't help herself. "What about your diet?"

"Oh." A guilty flush crept up Sarah's pale cheeks. "I

can't resist these scones. I'll burn it off on a bike ride tonight."

"You have a bike?" My, they were made to be friends.

"Can't afford a car just yet," Sarah admitted.

"Join the club," Abby snorted. Not that a car was particularly needed in a town this small. Still, when winter hit... "Why don't we meet this week and do our nails? Maybe get a glass of wine after?"

"I can do Wednesday," Sarah said.

Abby grinned. "Wednesday it is."

She patted the basket of scones and gave a side-eyed glance to the hall, where Zach was no doubt hard at work, trying to ruin someone else's day. Well, he wouldn't be ruining hers. Not today at least. After all, he'd ruined far too many already.

*

Zach shook his head as he spotted the basket of scones perched on top of Sarah's desk, but the smile slipped when he spotted Abby, laughing at something the receptionist was saying. Once there was a time when Abby's laugh was a constant fixture in his life, and something he'd probably taken for granted, not knowing just how much it meant until it was gone. He stopped walking, savoring the sound for just a moment, knowing that as soon as he appeared in the lobby all merriment would cease and the scowl would be back.

But he needed those files Sarah was supposed to be

organizing. Research for a lame article on the new renovation plans for the harbor that was due before the end of the day. He'd thought it would be easier to write about dull subjects, safe, relatable problems like the rotting wood down at the dock and the zoning committee's plans for it. But the novelty had worn off in a matter of days and now he was restless and confused as hell. He'd left his job. Told himself it was becoming too much, not just the travel but...the stories. They haunted him at night, made him anxious and unsettled. All those people he'd interviewed. All those people he couldn't help.

But this? Writing about country inn breakfasts and small-town construction? This wasn't him. But if this wasn't, then what?

He had time to figure that out, he supposed. Time that wasn't there before. Not when he was busy flying from the location of one world crisis to the next, covering the worst of humanity, seeing it firsthand instead of at a safe distance.

He turned to walk away before Abby spotted him, but it was too late.

"Zach?" Her voice was loud, and if he didn't know better, he'd go so far as to say there was a mocking quality to it.

He turned back, forcing a pleasant smile. Tried to look equally fake surprised at seeing her there. He hated these games. "Abby?"

Her lips pinched slightly, showing that she hadn't

bought his performance any more than he'd bought hers. She'd come to snuff him out, no doubt. The gossip had spread, as it always did in a town this small, and she'd discovered he was working here.

"You work here?" The knowing arch of her brow told him she already knew he did.

"That I do." Thrusting his hands into his pockets, he walked into the lobby, bracing himself for the inevitable tension. Sarah's gaze flicked to him, followed immediately by Abby's, and, after only a barely detectable hesitation, her face broke out into a wide grin that nearly boasted a dimple, which said a lot, considering Abby didn't have dimples.

"Oh do you now? Interesting. I'm surprised you didn't mention it before. Fresh *scone*?" she asked, holding up the basket like a slightly unhinged version of Martha Stewart. There was a bit of wild look to her eyes that he didn't like. Something that said she was onto him. "Baked fresh at the Harper House Inn less than an hour ago. They're still warm. Certainly not *dry*."

He felt uneasy and held up a hand. "I'm good."

"Oh, come on now, you don't want to hurt my feelings, do you?" While she maintained the hundred-watt smile, her eyes glimmered with challenge, as if daring him to deny her request.

He stifled a sigh and reached for a scone. "No," he said, honestly. "I wouldn't ever want to hurt your feelings." He locked her eyes, hoping to God she heard the sincerity in his tone, that he meant every word of that and always had. That it had nearly torn him apart when she left him that day, and that he'd replayed it over and over, each time the pain in his chest just as sharp as the last. But what choice had she given him? To come back here, to Oyster Bay? Give up on his dreams and work for the local paper?

The irony wasn't lost on him. Not one damn bit.

She turned away at that, her smile slipping enough for him to notice, but not enough for Sarah to catch on that something was amiss. Instead the receptionist wagged her finger in mock accusation and said, "Wait a minute. How do you two know each other?"

"We used to—" He started, and then, glancing her way, stopped. There were so many ways to finish that sentence. They used to date? Be in love? Be friends? Be happy?

Any and all of those responses were true.

"We went to the same college," Abby said tightly, refusing to meet his eye. "And Zach stayed on for grad school. Besides, in a town as small as Oyster Bay, you eventually know everyone."

"And run in to everyone," he added. This time it was his turn to give her a challenging look.

"How's the scone?" she asked, smiling again.

He hadn't tried it yet, but given the way both women were now staring at him, he could tell he wasn't in a position to delay. Obligingly, he took a bite and chewed it. Damn.

"That's a good scone," he said, giving her a nod of appreciation. Since when did Abby cook? Or bake? Back in college, she couldn't be bothered to boil water. She'd heat it up in the microwave instead. Her coffee was instant.

"Not...dry?" she asked pertly. "Not...*overly ambitious?*" Her smile was frozen on her face as she blinked up at him.

Great. She was quoting him, and not just quoting him, but quoting something he wasn't particularly proud of. A review of a so-so brunch. Could he even call that journalism? No. He couldn't. Not anymore than he could call his next piece an actual assignment.

She was watching, waiting, trying to break him down, the way she used to do back in college, when she wanted to go to the movies and he wanted to stay in and study. It was one of the things he'd loved about her and one of the things that had driven them apart. Abby was fun. He was serious. Abby was spontaneous and he was, well, not.

He pulled in a sigh and jutted his chin at Sarah. "It'll go great with a cup of coffee. Sarah, do you have the file on that zoning meeting?"

"A zoning meeting," Abby said slowly. "Are those the kind of topics you're covering now?"

He didn't respond, but instead looked at the receptionist. "Sarah?"

A guilty flush crept up Sarah's face. "I was just about to find that..."

"It's my fault," Abby said quickly, and Zach immediately knew that this was not the case at all. It was Abby, being Abby. She was kind that way, upbeat and cheerful and always looking to set everything right and keep the peace. He could still remember the time she invited his best friend to join them on their Valentine's Day date, claiming the guy looked too sad to be left alone and that they could always go out alone another night. Abby cared about others. She was a friend to all. Everyone except him now. "I kept her busy chatting, I'm afraid," she continued. The wink she tossed at Sarah was too obvious to go unnoticed.

"Well, we have work to do," he said, and his deadline was ticking away, a nagging reminder that gone were the days where he could pound out a story in a rush of adrenaline, fueled by excitement and a need to be heard. To make a difference.

He hadn't made a lick of difference. It had all been for nothing.

Abby was staring at him, her eyes stony, her mouth pinched. "Actually, I was here on official work business."

His eyes drifted to the basket, skeptically, and Abby must have followed his gaze. With a huff, she grabbed the basket. "And I should run now. See you Wednesday, Sarah."

Without so much as another look in his direction, she disappeared out through the front door, leaving Zach standing there with a half-eaten scone and a sudden longing to turn back time. Long past the decision to write that stupid review. But further, way back, when Abby was still his and that smile was still meant for him.

Chapter Seven

As she did every day since the review came out, Abby started her morning by checking the paper, to see if her plan had worked. By Wednesday, as with every day, she was deflated to see that it hadn't. So far.

Still, she did have the satisfaction of seeing Zach eat her scone and enjoy it. She'd proven him wrong, shown him what she could do, that she could make something of herself too. Right here in Oyster Bay.

She set the paper to the side with a sigh and went back to cracking eggs for today's special—garden omelets—when she saw Bridget out of the corner of her eye. She couldn't help it: her heart sped up and her mouth went dry and she was actually scared. Scared of her own sister. More scared than she'd been when she was nine and she'd stolen Bridget's new lipstick and given her dolls a makeover and then left the tube on the radiator to melt.

She dared to look up, knowing somehow from her strong reaction that she had reason to worry. Bridget wasn't smiling. In fact, she looked worried.

"Everything okay?" Abby asked lightly, even though her voice was a little shrill and her chest was positively pounding now. Was this it? The end of her trial period? Had Bridget decided the risk wasn't worth it, that she was better off with fresh fruit and coffee and pastries delivered from Angie's each morning in crisp white boxes?

"We just had a cancellation for this weekend," Bridget said. Peak season, no less.

Abby wondered if the panic registered on her face. She cracked another egg, buying time, wondering if she should say something or nothing and which was worse.

She never could keep quiet for long. "Any particular reason why?"

"Nope." Bridget walked over to the coffee machine. "Just a cancellation."

Surely that wasn't unheard of. Maybe the person got sick or maybe something came up at work. Or maybe they read the review of her dry and burnt scones and decided to take their money elsewhere!

Her hands were shaking as she cracked the last egg. There was nothing more to keep her hands busy. She'd whisk.

Bridget shrugged. "It's strange, summer season and

all." She looked out the window, onto the patio, where a few guests had already gathered with their coffees, and Abby felt the weight of disappointment on her shoulders. It could never be proven, of course they'd never know, but she knew, in her heart of hearts, she just knew. Even if the person hadn't read the review or canceled because of it, Bridget was thinking the same thing as her.

And that just meant that she had to do something to turn that impression around. And fast.

Two batches of fresh scones to the offices of the *Oyster Bay Gazette* was yet to achieve the results she had wanted, and the second batch had ended up in a plastic container, ready for her next trip to Serenity Hills, which would probably be tomorrow. Should she go for a third batch, and a fourth, maybe swap them out for her famous chocolate chip muffins (well, they were famous at Serenity Hills, especially amongst the toothless crowd, who claimed they simply melted in your mouth) or her double fudge brownies?

Or should she lie low, act like she didn't care? Or should she send an invitation to dine at the inn again, to give it another try?

She'd decided on her bike ride to the inn that morning that the latter option would never work. The entire point of the pseudonym was that the reviewer was supposed to be anonymous. An acceptance of an invitation would make things all too clear too quickly. Though it would of course confirm what she already knew to be true.

Zach. How could he do it? Why did he do it? To

punish her? Sure, he hadn't known she was the cook at the time, but it was her family business, and her family home.

She narrowed her eyes just thinking about it, and she didn't even realize she was still scowling until Bridget looked over at her, frowning. "Everything okay?"

"What?" Abby felt her cheeks heat. "Oh, just dropped a shell into the eggs."

Stupid thing to say, Abby! Now you really look incompetent.

Bridget stood there for a moment and then said, "Well, I'd better go see if anyone needs anything before I run Emma over to camp. They're making macaroni necklaces today," she added with a grin.

Abby grinned back. Her face felt frozen and on fire all at once. She didn't breathe again until her sister was gone.

She couldn't live like this much longer. Time to get things back on track. And fast.

*

Sarah looked up from the bench outside the nail salon where they had agreed to meet, her expression alarmed.

"Is everything okay?" she asked.

Was it that obvious she was so distressed? Abby shook the newfound worry from this morning free from her mind. This evening was supposed to be about fun, a chance to escape her troubles for a few hours and have some laughs with a new friend. She couldn't think of the last time she'd done something like this.

"Everything is just fine," she said. Or it would be, and soon if she had anything to do with it.

The girls entered the salon, which served hair at the back and nails at the front, the one that Abby had worked at a couple years back, washing hair and barely collecting enough tips to make ends meet. It had been fun at first—the girl talk, the casual environment—but there was only so much scalp you could stare at, only so many tendrils you could run your fingers through before a challenge was needed.

That challenge had been the insurance agency. She idly wondered how Fred was doing. Was he still passionately explaining the benefits of a high-deductible plan? Had her waxy plant survived?

"Did you happen to talk to your grandmother today?" Sarah asked after they'd chosen their colors (carnation pink for Sarah and robin's egg blue for Abby) and settled into side-by-side massage chairs.

Abby didn't like the ominous tone the question took on. "No. Why?"

"Well." Sarah dragged out the word and gave her a long look. "There was an incident in the garden courtyard."

"An incident? As in something of a food fight variety?" She immediately envisioned petals strewn and tempers flaring.

Sarah waggled her eyebrows. "It seems that my grandmother accused your grandmother of picking some flowers."

A major offense at Serenity Hills. Sweet little Emma had once reached for a lovely pale pink tulip only to be scolded by a widower from the third floor, who had three snarly teeth and a penchant for calling women under the age of eighty "Missy."

"Don't you go picking that flower, Missy," he'd cried out, and it had taken poor Emma a moment to realize he was addressing her and not someone named, well, Missy. "Don't you see that sign?"

Indeed there was a sign, which he tapped firmly with his cane, tucked at the corner of the garden, under a weeping willow, very easy to miss.

Abby had bit her tongue, taken Emma, who seemed confused and on the brink of tears, by the hand, and promised to buy her a lovely pink tulip from the flower shop later that day.

And now it would seem Mimi had made the same offense. Their family was on the verge of developing quite a reputation.

"Go on," Abby urged as she plunged her feet into the warm bubbling water. Rose petals floated on top and Abby wondered why she didn't treat herself to this type of thing more often.

Oh, that's right. Because stuff like this cost money. And bouncing between jobs didn't really allow for much savings.

All the more reason to keep the good thing she had going. And, hopefully, grow it.

"My grandmother called the police."

"The police!" As every face in the room swiveled to stare at her, Abby realized she had said that too loudly. She leaned into Sarah. "Why didn't she just call security?"

"I don't think she felt security did enough with...well, what your niece did," Sarah said with a shrug.

Oh, for God's sake! Word traveled faster in Serenity Hills than it did down Main Street!

"They didn't arrest her, did they?" Abby was suddenly alarmed, picturing her grandmother sitting in a cement jail cell with a tray of lukewarm soup and a rock-hard bread roll. Then she remembered that her brother-in-law was the sheriff and that there was no way Eddie would have taken her in.

And God knew that Mimi would have put up a fight if he'd tried.

"Apparently the head of the facility was called in and there was a lot of arguing. Your grandmother denied cutting the flower but was reprimanded for it anyway, and mine was scolded for involving the police instead of just reporting things to the front desk. My grandmother was quite disappointed in the outcome." Sarah clucked her tongue and both women started to laugh.

"I don't know what she's more disappointed in," Sarah continued as she idly flicked a page in her magazine. "That Margaret Harper wasn't kicked out of Serenity Hills or that I am still single."

"You're getting the pressure too?" Abby rolled her eyes. "Tell me about it. Even my grandmother is getting married. My sisters are both divorced, but somehow they think I'm the one that struggles in relationships. Please tell me how that makes any sense?"

Sarah shook her head. "I'm an only child. All eyes are on me to settle down and deliver the grandchildren. It's why I moved to Oyster Bay, actually. The excuse was to be closer to my grandmother, but I really needed some space from my parents."

"I understand." Well, not the parents part. Always an awkward topic. She decided to dodge it today, leave the heavier stuff for another time. When a glass of wine was involved, preferably. Or maybe, never. Maybe Sarah could learn that tidbit through the Serenity Hills gossip mill. It was too hard to go to back to that time and place, when her world changed.

"No luck in the old town?"

"No luck in general," Sarah sighed. "I'm kind of a pariah with men."

"You?" Abby laughed. "But you're so pretty." With her blonde hair and Barbie doll figure, Abby struggled to see the problem.

"I've been told I come on too strong," Sarah admitted. She chewed her bottom lip before explaining, "I made a big mistake with the last guy who took me out to dinner."

Abby stared at her, so riveted that she almost didn't notice when her foot was lifted into the air and the bottom was pumiced smooth, something that usually made her writhe.

"What did you do?"

"I called him. To thank him for dinner."

"Well, that's a polite thing to do." Sure, she wasn't playing hard to get, but that wasn't exactly eager either.

"I called him before work. On his landline. Assuming that he would have left for the day. And that I could just leave a message." Sarah looked at her imploringly. "I called him at seven fifteen in the morning. And he answered. And he thought I was crazy."

Oh, boy. Yes, Sarah had a lot to learn when it came to the dating scene, not that Abby would classify herself as an expert.

"And the one before him?"

Abby blinked. There were others? "Yes?" she asked, though she wasn't sure she wanted to know.

"He was a friend. Well, I was a friend to him. But I'd always wanted it to be something more. And…" She looked so distressed that Abby considered stopping her, but it was clear that this was something Sarah had to get off her chest. "I wrote him an email, professing my feelings."

Abby didn't need to hear the end of the story to know how it finished.

"It was the second time I'd done that, actually."

"With the same guy?" Abby cried.

"Of course not. Two different guys. Same outcome, though," Sarah added, heaving a long sigh.

"Well, the nice thing about being new to town is that everyone is a fresh face," Abby said to encourage her, even if the same argument couldn't be used to lift her own spirits. "I've seen most of these guys since they were playing Little League."

"Like Zach?"

Something in the way Sarah said his name made Abby freeze. She stared at her new friend, realizing her heart was pumping in her chest. There was a light in Sarah's eyes. An eagerness that bordered on hope.

"Zach and I used to date, actually," she said a little tightly.

Sarah blinked in surprise. "Oh. I didn't know."

Abby's breathing was heavy. She could brush it off, make it out to be the ancient history that it was—a brief, fleeting moment in time—but she couldn't. Not anymore than she could think about Zach moving on, or Sarah— or anyone else—having a possible interest in him.

"Well, it didn't come up," she said a little huffily. God, she really hated herself for that comment. She turned back to the magazine and flicked a page.

Were they about to have a Mimi and Esther moment? Was water from the basin about to be splashed, nail polish flung?

"I sort of like the guy he sits next to," Sarah said, to Abby's extreme relief.

She smiled, a smile that she shouldn't feel, even if she did, from her soaring heart all the way down to the tips of her toes, which now happily wiggled in the water.

"What's his name?" she asked with interest.

"Brad," Sarah sighed and leaned her head back on the chair, closing her eyes.

Abby went through her mental rolodex of old classmates and tried to recall the photo of the *Gazette* staff she'd snapped that first time she'd dropped off scones. "Not Brad Norris?"

"Yes!" Sarah's eyes were so wide that Abby could see the whites all around her eyes. "Isn't he cute?"

Abby stopped to consider this. She'd never really thought about it before, never properly looked. She still thought of Brad as the kid who used to toss rolled up scraps of paper into the brim of Mrs. Hernandez's sombrero in first year Spanish. The teacher insisted on wearing that thing, and every time she turned around, Brad scored another basket, eliciting a snicker from the other boys and a curl of the lip from most of the girls. Still, Abby supposed he had grown up since seventh grade. At least a little. "Why don't you ask him to show you around town?"

Sarah looked horror stricken at the mere thought. "I'm too afraid to talk to him." Suddenly her eyes burst open and she leaned forward, "Hey, I have a great idea! You and Zach could invite me and Brad out one night!"

Abby frowned. That's what Sarah called a great idea? That was what Abby called a recipe for disaster.

"Oh, I don't know…"

"It will be perfect. We can make it look casual. And you're so outgoing, Abby, you can help me to open up!" Sarah looked so desperate that Abby wasn't quite sure how she could say no to her new friend.

She chewed her bottom lip, considering her options. A night out with Zach might help win him over a bit, or make him feel guilty enough to rewrite the article. But it wouldn't rewrite history, she reminded herself. She'd have to keep her emotions in check. Keep it brief. Get out of there once Sarah and Brad had formed a love connection.

"I don't know if Zach would go along with it," she said in all honesty.

"Oh, I just thought you seemed okay with each other at the office," Sarah said, looking disappointed that her grand plan wasn't so great. "Did you guys have a really bad break up?"

Define bad, Abby thought. If bad meant that she had packed up every single thing in her dorm that had ever belonged to him and left them with the doorman of his apartment building, then yes, it was bad. If bad meant that said doorman had then reached below his desk and pulled out a Macy's shopping bag, stuffed full of her belongings, his grey eyes saying "sorry" even though his mouth said nothing, then yes, it was bad.

If by bad Sarah meant that when Abby started crying when Zach told her his plans, and when it was clear he wouldn't budge, and that they were over, he had tried to comfort her by saying, "Abby, it's not like I'm dead" and her tears had all at once stopped and she had hissed at him on her way out the door "You're dead to me" then yes, it had ended badly.

And if that was the last thing she ever said to him until the morning he appeared on the porch of the inn, then yes. Their break up had been very, very, very bad.

"It's okay, I don't want to put you out." Sarah went back to her magazine, and Abby knew she could let it go, accept the relief with getting out of a social situation she didn't want to be a part of.

But, damn it... "No, it's fine. We're cool." Ha! "I'll ask him next time I see him." Whenever that would be. Zach hadn't been in town long and she seemed to be running into him every other day. And then there were those visits to the paper, of course...

"Oh, thank you, Abby! Thank you! I mean, I'm a disaster at dating, really, like meeting people isn't my strong suit now that my confidence is so shaken. But with you there...Oh, this is going to be so much fun!"

Fun? Abby could think of a few other choice words to describe how things would go. Fun was not at the top of the list.

Still, she'd find a way to use the evening to her advantage. Zach already liked her scones. Now all she had to do was find a way to get him to write a glowing review that would push the other into the dust.

*

By the time the girls had left the salon, their toenails and fingernails perfectly painted, on display for all of the tourists to see, Abby was feeling refreshed. She hadn't even thought about the cancellation or the review or

Bridget...until she saw the cover of the newspaper at the corner newsstand, and then it all came flooding back like some terrible dream.

"Oh, look! A festival!" Sarah gestured to a leaflet that was tacked to a tree.

Abby curled her lip. When she was little, she found endless delight in these local traditions, and as an adult, she went, because everyone went, and it was something to do, but now all she could think of was that a festival was just another place to bump into Zach, when what she really wanted was some distance. Once her mission was accomplished, she'd go out of her way to avoid him. That is, if he wasn't gone first.

Her heart tugged a little at that thought.

"Oyster Bay loves its festivals. They have like six a year. Not that they aren't fun, but if you can think of a reason for a town event, you can pretty much assume that it's already being planned."

"Do they take volunteers?" Sarah asked.

"I'm sure," she said, not giving it much thought. After all, someone had to hang the decorations and organize the tables and kid events.

"Would you sign up with me?" Sarah asked. "It might be a good way to meet people, and besides, it would be fun."

There was that word again, but here was a situation where Abby agreed. And right now, she could use a little fun. "Okay, then. I'll look into when the next meeting is and we can go together."

Something in the way Sarah lit up made Abby wonder if she was hoping that some cute guys might be in attendance. As if. Those things were always run by the town bosses, in other words, retired teachers, general busybodies, and young moms looking for a reason to escape. The only time the men were involved was when their wives signed them up to do the heavy lifting.

Abby grinned at this. Maybe she'd volunteer to do something that required a tool belt. Shake things up a bit.

"I have an idea," she said, as they approached Dunley's. Out of loyalty to Bridget, she didn't frequent the place as often as she'd like to, but her sister didn't mind the occasional visit, especially when she reported back her observations. Ryan had a revolving door of girlfriends that Bridget had seemed keen on hearing about, even if did make her complexion go all ruddy and her eyes all squinty and her mouth all pinched. Abby always felt guilty in those moments, wondering if she should have refused to feed into Bridget's request or play dumb, but then she reminded herself that he was Emma's father, and as her mother, Bridget did have reason to wonder who was spending time with her daughter. Still… She hated to hurt Bridget's feelings. She could only hope that Bridget felt the same way about her.

Come to think of it, though, now that Bridget had Jack in her life, she didn't seem as concerned about Ryan's extracurricular activities.

"Do you have time for a drink?" Knowing the answer

to that, she said, "This place is always full of singles, especially the ones who just come for the summer. And there's usually some cute guys behind the bar, too. Why don't you use this as a practice run for talking to Brad?"

Immediately, she sensed Sarah hesitate. "Oh, no. I don't think that's a good idea."

"Why not? Because you're afraid you wouldn't know what to say?"

"Exactly." Sarah looked downright scared, and before she could flee the scene, Abby grabbed her by the wrist and pulled her into the bar, which was loud and energetic and a big departure from the serenity of the salon.

Just what they needed, she thought. Well, especially Sarah.

Sarah, being Sarah, started walking over to an empty table, but Abby shook her head. "We're here to chat with guys, not each other. We're going to sit at the bar."

"I don't do bars."

"Then what do you do? Online dating?" If Sarah thought she was going to find love volunteering for the Summer Fest, Abby could personally guarantee her that wasn't going to happen. In fact, she would sooner shave her eyebrows than put money on finding any sort of romantic possibility at that festival.

"I have online dated before, yes," Sarah said, as Abby shifted her over to the left side of the bar, away from the group of single women at the right side. She spotted Amanda Quinn across the room and gave a weary wave.

You really couldn't go anywhere in Oyster Bay without running into someone you knew. Or in this case, someone Zach dated.

Zach and Amanda had been high school sweethearts, gone to prom together and everything, long before Abby really noticed Zach or gave him much consideration. Their age gap didn't close off until college, and by then, Amanda was in beauty school, pursuing her dreams of opening her own spa one day. That day had come about five years ago when Amanda and her best friend Rachel went into business together, opening Chez Moi, an exclusive day spa at the edge of town that featured seaweed wraps, mud baths, and waxing...of all the parts.

Abby turned away from Amanda. The very single, very pretty Amanda, with her perky smile and expertly applied makeup, who was likely all too happy that Zach Dillon was back in town, looking just as good as ever. So maybe they'd get back together. It could happen. And would Abby care?

Sadly, she would.

"And how did that go? The online dating?" Her eyes kept flitting back to Amanda, who seemed engrossed in a conversation with Rachel, and Abby tried really hard to read her lips, to see if they were talking about...Oh, this was really ridiculous now.

"Well, the first guy I really connected with over emails. But when we met in real life I realized that I actually outweighed him by a solid fifteen pounds."

Abby raked her eyes over Sarah's slender frame. "How

is that even possible?"

"Exactly." Sarah bit her lip. "But that wasn't the problem, not really. The problem was that he spent the entire dinner talking about his last girlfriend, and then at the end of the night told me that they'd only broken up a week ago. He said he hadn't eaten since."

"Sounds like you dodged a bullet there," Abby said, chuckling.

"And then there was the next date..." Sarah shook her head, as if remembering. "He looked like his picture, which was good. But he was very evasive about his past. And it wasn't until the dessert came that I realized he'd just been released from prison."

"Prison!"

"A white-collar crime...I did give him one more try."

Abby looked at her in fascination. "And then you realized that you couldn't date an ex-con?"

Sarah shook her head. "Then I realized he had a tendency to talk too much. About his time. About those years. And well, I was tired of listening and not talking, too. Plus, he had a habit of checking out every woman that walked by. Said he couldn't help himself, that his only eye candy in lockdown was a sixty-five-year-old security guard name Maria."

Laughing, Abby slid onto her barstool and smiled at the, okay, fairly cute bartender, even if he was about five years too young for her, which was a bit of a strange thought. Clearly Ryan was using seasonal help to offset the crowd, which was large, especially for a Wednesday night. "Two glasses of house white," she said, and then, deciding to use this as a teaching moment, batted her eyes and said, "Unless you have a better suggestion?"

Sure enough, the bartender grinned, rather suggestively if Abby didn't know better, and with a mysterious lift of one eyebrow, began pouring and shaking and then sliding two bright pink drinks in front of them, complete with umbrellas.

"Have a name for this?" Abby asked, admiring the concoction.

"Two Pretty Girls Walked into a Bar," the guy replied, before turning to a set of customers who had just arrived. Abby laughed, in surprise, in delight. It had been a long time since she'd done this. Well, since Chase followed his band to Florida back in the fall.

She suddenly remembered how it felt. Good. Distracting.

And shallow, she realized with an inward frown. There was no depth to these types of interactions. Just fun. And she'd been all about fun for a very long time.

"When he comes back, it's your turn," Abby said.

Sarah looked panicked. "Oh no. I can't."

Abby tapped her new friend's glass. "Have a few sips of that. It will help. But don't have too many. That won't help you either."

Sarah dutifully took a sip from her drink. "It's good!"

"Tell him that," Abby said, jutting her chin at the bartender, whose back was still to them.

"I…I…" At this moment, the bartender turned toward them and flashed a hundred-watt grin.

Abby elbowed Sarah. Maybe a tad too hard, given the way she wobbled on her stool for a moment.

"It's good," Sarah said, smiling from overt nerves, but still, smiling all the same.

The bartender just winked and turned to help another customer.

"He winked at me!" Sarah looked astonished. Abby didn't have the heart to tell her that it didn't mean anymore than the silly name he'd given the drinks. The man was a professional flirt, a seasonal bartender hired no doubt on account of his looks and outgoing personality, strategically placed to keep the ladies coming back and ordering drinks. Ryan was a suave businessman. "You must date a lot to be so good at this."

Date a lot. Abby supposed she did, but thinking of it that way didn't sit right.

The girls sipped their drinks and chatted about their grandmothers until Sarah started to yawn. "Well," she sighed, "I suppose I should head out. I need my beauty rest for tomorrow morning." Her eyes twinkled. "It does sort of make work more fun when there's something to look forward to, though, you know what I mean?"

Abby did, only in her case, it wasn't the prospect of seeing a cute guy tomorrow morning at work that made her heart do a little dance. It was the thought of doing what she loved, what she believed in, and following her heart.

And hopefully…making it last this time.

*

Zach sat in the dining room of his childhood home, an old, yellow painted Cape with black shutters on the far north side of town, and stared at the food in front of him, thinking how little had changed. His first week back, his mother fell back on all his old favorites: roasted turkey with mashed potatoes, and spaghetti with meatballs. Tonight it was chicken parmesan. It made him a little sad, thinking of how his palette has evolved in recent years, while here in Oyster Bay life felt almost frozen in time.

Melanie sat across from him, in the same chair she'd always sat in for special occasions. He supposed his presence called for use of the formal dining room instead of the solid oak kitchen table, and it made him feel shifty. He should have come home more often, should have stopped by for holidays, at least. But there was always a story, an opportunity, a reason to stay away.

Their mother took a deep breath. "So Melly."

Across the table, Melanie's eyes shot up to his. She hated to be called Melly. Said it made her feel like she was ten years old again. Also, there had been the whole "Smelly Melly" nickname at one point when puberty first kicked in.

"Anything new?" There was nothing casual about her tone.

"Just work and home," Melanie shrugged, decidedly

evasive. "We just saw the new fall line of dresses. It's amazing how many brides are opting for long sleeves!"

Zach had tried to talk to his sister on the way over here, to get a casual feel for what was going on in her life, but she'd been determined to keep the conversation neutral, talking only about the bridal salon where she worked and the latest trends in bridesmaid dresses. Now she gave him a look that said he owed her. After all, he'd begged her to come to this dinner, hoping that it would take some of the pressure off of himself, that it would keep his mother from asking the tough questions that he didn't want to answer.

So far, the plan wasn't working.

"Any dates?" His mother coyly stabbed a spear of broccoli and brought it to her mouth while Melanie fumed.

"So, Dad," Zach cut in, eager not to get on his sister's bad side. "How's work?"

"I should be asking you that. How are things going at the *Gazette*?"

How were things going? They weren't. Unless you counted the occasional surprise visit from Abby, there was little to be excited about most days. It wouldn't last. He knew himself and he knew it wouldn't sustain him. But he wouldn't tell his parents that. Not tonight, at least.

"Fine," he said, shoveling some food into his mouth so he had reason not to elaborate.

"Have you gotten out with any of your friends?" his

mother pressed.

Not unless Abby counted. And Brad was good for a drink or two. He supposed he could look up some old pals from high school, but that felt like a lifetime ago. Many were married by now. A few even had kids. He couldn't relate, and he doubted they could relate to him either.

Without waiting for a reply, his mother said, "Well, I've taken the liberty of signing you both up as volunteers for the Summer Fest."

"What?" Melanie looked even more horrified than Zach felt, only he was too polite to show his true feelings. Too much time had passed. He felt formal sitting here against the stiff, hardback chair, that hardly ever had any use, aside from Christmas and Thanksgiving and the occasional visit from his father's mother, whom his own mother was forever trying to impress and had never managed to.

"It will do you good to get involved, and we need all the help we can get." His mother gave Melanie a stern look, the kind she used to give when Melanie was twelve and protesting over doing her homework when her favorite show was on.

"I don't have to time to get involved," Melanie said, her tone unapologetic. "I have...responsibilities."

She flashed him a look that now said he had better not dare to contradict that statement. After all, what were these responsibilities? Keeping the ratings high for the struggling soaps and a string of reality dating shows? His mother was right; it would do Melanie good to get out of the house and be involved.

And only for that reason he said, "I'll do it if Melanie does."

He didn't need to look at his sister now to know that she was positively glaring at him. Any glance in her direction would result in a stare-down, and unlike when they were kids, he didn't suspect it would end in laughter when someone blinked first.

"Then it's settled." His mother was beaming. His father just shook his head. "Won't it be nice to have something to do on a Friday night?"

She looked pointedly at Melanie, who stayed eerily silent. Zach knew he had it coming to him. But for once, it didn't matter.

He couldn't change the world, much as he'd tried. But he could help his sister out. At least until she evicted him.

Chapter Eight

On late Friday afternoon, Abby hopped off her bike and propped it against a sturdy maple outside of Town Hall, one of the town's prettiest brick buildings in all of Oyster Bay, right in the center of town. She looked down the street, past the shops and awnings and park benches flanked by potted hydrangeas that were bursting with shades of blue and periwinkle. There was no sign of Sarah, but considering Abby was five minutes late, she might have already gone ahead inside.

With one last look around, Abby hurried up the steps, pulled open the front door, and followed the signs to the Festival Planning Committee meeting at the end of the long hall, thinking that really, she'd rather be down at the beach with a good book, or sitting in front of a chick flick with a cold glass of wine right about now. Or trying out recipes for Mimi's wedding cake. Mimi was partial to chocolate, but a lemon chiffon would be so refreshing!

Still, it was good to be involved. And it would be something to take her mind of her worries about work and—

Oh, for God's sake!

"Hey there, Abby." Zach sauntered over to her, grin on his face, glint in his eye. He was dressed as if he'd come straight from the office, in khakis and a button down blue shirt that was rolled at the sleeves. Melanie hovered behind him, arguing with their mother, her eyes darting around the room. A family affair, it would seem.

She narrowed her hold on him, desperately wishing she had already spotted Sarah when she'd first entered the room.

"I'm meeting a friend," she said, trying to sidestep him. "I should really find her. She's waiting for me."

"Sarah said to tell you she's running late."

Her lids drooped. "Sarah knew you would be here?" A heads-up would have been nice. A little warning so she could have put more thought into what she was wearing. Not that it mattered. Not that Zach probably cared. And really, a skirt and tee were fine, even if the hem of the shirt was a little threadbare.

"She mentioned at work that she was coming here tonight, and I mentioned that my mom is head of the planning committee this year." He cocked an eyebrow. "So you don't need to worry that I followed you here or something."

The ass. "I didn't."

But now it looked like she had followed him here, when, in fact, Sarah hadn't breathed a word.

"Sarah invited me to come. Wednesday," she clarified. "She's new in town and she thought this would be a good way to meet people. And since I'm from here and I know everyone, I offered to join her."

And now she was over explaining. A true sign of guilt. Even when she was guilty of nothing.

Zach raised another eyebrow but didn't say a word. He had always been good at that—listening and retaining but not replying, not giving an opinion one way or another. It was what made him such a good journalist, no doubt.

"I'm not following you, for your information," she huffed, eager to make that clear.

He had the nerve to give a little grin. "I never said you were."

"No, but you were thinking it." He was always thinking, and his thoughts were always revealed. If not verbally, then in his writing, in his slant. Oh no, he hadn't bothered to complain about the burnt scone or ask for another. Instead he had absorbed what was given to him and then...Well. She was getting worked up again. Her breathing was heavy. And this really wasn't the place for it.

The grin widened. Just a notch. "You come by my office...I see you at Jojo's..."

"I was at Jojo's first," she reminded him. "And this is a

small town."

"Abby Harper!" Dottie Joyce took that moment to croon. She grabbed Abby by the wrist, her clutch so firm that Abby had to refrain from wincing in pain.

"Hello, Mrs. Joyce," she said weakly. Dottie had always been a nosy sort, the kind of woman who made it her business to know your business. Most people had made a habit of crossing the street when they saw her coming. Ever since Margo redecorated Dottie's house last fall, Dottie had it in her head that she had a special connection to the Harpers. And tonight Abby was the only one in attendance.

"It's so nice to see you here tonight." Her eyes widened a notch when she saw Zach. "And Zach Dillon. I *heard* you were back in town. Your mother's fit to be tied, you know." She gave an exaggerated wink, like she and Zach were in on some sort of conspiracy.

Abby felt bad for him. Almost.

"I see that you and Abby have reunited then!" She nodded her head, as if giving this her official approval. As head of the Historical Society, she took her interest in local history to include the personal lives of all the residents.

Abby exchanged a look with Zach, thinking that she'd let him take this one. It would be fun to see him squirm a bit.

"It's certainly nice catching up with old friends while I'm back in Oyster Bay," he said pleasantly, but Abby knew him well enough to detect the hint of impatience in his eyes.

"*While* you're back!" Dottie looked alarmed. "You mean, you aren't staying?"

"I'm at a crossroads for the moment," he said a little stiffly. Abby was aware that her chest was pounding as she stared at him, waiting for him to elaborate, a little afraid of what he might say. "I'm not sure what the next step is."

Dottie was blinking rapidly, trying to absorb this information, which was clearly opposing the gossip she'd gleaned around town. "Well. I...I...I hope that your mother won't be crushed!"

Zach shrugged. "As I said, I don't have a firm plan at the moment."

Abby frowned. Since when didn't Zach have a firm plan? Zach didn't do spontaneous, not when it came to his future, not when it came to his career. From the time he was twenty-two years old, he had a plan. He was going to intern at the *Boston Globe*, graduate with honors, and go to work for the biggest paper in the country.

She'd never thought to ask where she fit into those plans. She'd just assumed she was a part of them. Well, she'd assumed wrong.

"And nice to see Melanie here, too. Poor thing." Dottie clucked her tongue, and now it was Zach's turn to frown.

"Excuse me?" he asked, but Dottie wasn't listening to him anymore. Her attention was firmly returned to Abby.

Abby stifled a sigh. Where was Sarah?

"So then. What made you decide to finally get involved?"

Abby caught Zach's smug grin from the corner of her eye and felt her own mouth thin. "A friend invited me," she told Dottie.

"And there's the friend now!" Zach said loudly, practically pushing her toward the door. There was no denying the heat that rushed down her spine at the feel of his hands on her shoulders, the strong grip of them, and the comfort of their warmth. She could have kissed him in that moment, not because he'd touched her, reminded her, but because he'd saved her.

Sure enough, there was Sarah, her hair tied up in a ponytail, her eyes scanning the crowd, no doubt hopeful that if Zach was near, Brad might be too.

She was going to be mighty disappointed. So far the only other man in attendance was poor old Wally Jennings, whose wife insisted he come everywhere with her, even though she was forever bossing him around and making him hold her shopping bags. "Yes, Martha" was his nickname around town, because that's what he could be heard muttering all up and down Main Street.

Abby shook her head. The poor guy. He was a sweet sort. He reminded her of her grandfather, even though she'd never known either of her grandfathers, but he reminded her of how Mimi had described her late husband, at least.

Mimi. She made a mental note that Margo had called her about their bridesmaid dress fitting next weekend. Abby could only hope that Mimi would let them each choose their own style, or at the very least nothing would have puffed sleeves or a giant bow on the tailbone.

"I didn't miss anything, did I?" Sarah asked.

Not unless she counted another tense exchange with Zach as something to miss.

"Nope, nothing. Now, let's go get a seat," she started to move, but Zach took a step to his right, blocking her. She sensed the merriment in his expression and pinched her lips tight. So this was fun for him, was it? Teasing her, taunting her, showing up everywhere she went, drudging up memories she'd wanted to forget.

"Sarah was telling me you had the idea of a double date," Zach said, his eyes dancing when they met hers.

Well, Christ. He'd been holding onto that gem all this time, waiting for just the right moment to let it slip, no doubt thinking the entire time that Abby was, indeed, eager to spend time with him.

Hardly. The only thing she was eager for was a retraction on the article he still hadn't admitted to writing.

Abby glared sidelong at Sarah, who held up her hands helplessly, and gave a pleading smile. Yep, no help there.

"I thought it might be a nice way for Sarah to meet some people in Oyster Bay," Abby said coolly.

"But she already knows you, and Brad and I work with her." He wasn't going to make this easy for her. In fact, if she didn't know better, she might say he was determined to argue. He thrust his hands into his pockets, grinning in a rather cocky way that was—damn it—way more appealing than it should be. Did he still have to be so good looking? Couldn't all that traveling have aged him a bit more? Receded his hair line and given him a stomach paunch?

Abby darted her gaze to Sarah, who had decided at that moment to walk over to the coffee bar that was set up in the far corner of the room. Melanie was snacking on some cookies that Abby recognized from Angie's. Dry. In need of a pinch of salt to break up the sweetness. Why hadn't she thought to offer something?

"Is Brad single?" Abby asked, deciding to get to the point.

Zach blinked at her, then stared for a long time. "Hell if I know," he said, his voice gruff.

What kind of answer was that? But then, seeing the pinch of his brow, Abby realized... he was jealous. He thought that she was interested in Brad and he was jealous.

And she...loved it.

A little smile twisted at her lips, and something in her stomach did a little flutter. She knew she could correct him, set him straight and find out if poor Sarah stood a chance in heck with her coworker or if this little double date would end in heartbreak.

But then, by luck, or perhaps good old-fashioned fate, there was a rustling of chairs and a shushing off the crowd and a woman—Zach's mother to be exact—was calling the meeting to order.

Shame.

With a little smile back at Zach, Abby found Sarah in a row of chairs, front and center to her displeasure, and took her seat. She felt every eye in the place on her back, no doubt connecting her presence with Zach's. She half considered asking to take the floor just to silence all speculation from the start.

"Zach agreed to us all meeting for drinks tomorrow night," Sarah said, her voice lifted with hope.

"So I heard," Abby said. She didn't have the heart to tell her friend that Zach thought she was the one who was interested in Brad. That could be sorted out later. Right now she had more pressing concerns, like the fact that she kept catching Zach's profile in her periphery, because he was sitting across the aisle from her, next to Melanie, who looked bored and unhappy. Zach, on the other hand, seemed pumped up and agitated. He was sitting straight in his chair, fingers tented on his lap, his eyes fixed on the front of the room, his jaw tight.

Yep. Jealous. Oh, the sweet satisfaction.

"First order of business," Karen Dillon said, scanning the room and, by the smile that formed on her mouth, clearly pleased by the turnout. Both Zach and Melanie took after her, with their rich dark hair that contrasted their sharp blue eyes. "Food trucks. At the fall fest, we had a good turnout, with most restaurants or shops in town putting out a limited menu. I'd like to see if we could build on that, maybe get a few more options this time around."

Sarah elbowed her and stage whispered, "You should do one!"

Abby frowned. "A food truck? No, I don't think so." She wouldn't even know where to begin. What did you cook on, a hot plate? She couldn't bake in a toaster oven.

"Why not? You could represent the inn," Sarah urged.

Abby chewed her bottom lip. Actually, that wasn't a half-bad idea, and the festival always got plenty of coverage in the newspaper. A good review of her food in a public setting might offset that nasty review that the man who was currently looking at her with a raised eyebrow had written.

Keen as he was to deny that. Still, she'd drag it out of him. One way or another.

She glanced at him straight on, catching his stare, and gave him a friendly smile, even if she didn't feel friendly. She felt mad, downright angry that he thought she still cared enough to set up some double date. Please! As if! If anyone was pursuing anyone in this equation it was him.

She frowned. No. He wouldn't. Why bother? He'd said his piece a long time ago. He wasn't coming back to Oyster Bay. They didn't want the same things.

And yet here he was.

Messing up all her plans. Rattling her. Ruining her reputation and threatening the life she'd built for herself.

Well! She'd show him.

Without hesitation, she held up her arm and said, "The Harper House Inn would like to participate."

There. She settled back in her seat, finding it a bit hard, and felt a swell of panic rise in her chest.

She'd just volunteered to share her food with the public. A much bigger crowd than those who ever frequented the inn for weekend brunch. Could she face the possibility of more rejection, more criticism?

Looked like it was a risk she was going to have to take.

*

"Well, so much for finding any cute guys in there," Sarah remarked as they pushed through the doors of Town Hall ninety minutes later, each mentally armed with their volunteer assignments. Sarah would head up the kid's corner, making sure that crafts and games flowed smoothly, and Abby was asked to help with setup of the festival, something that took place the Sunday before the big event, leaving her the rest of the week to prepare for the food truck.

There was marked disappointment in her tone, but Abby wasn't ready to let her give up just yet. "We still have the date, I mean, the evening with Zach and Brad," she corrected herself. It wasn't a date, even if Zach had used the term.

Seriously, what had he meant by that? A double date with Sarah and Brad? In his dreams.

"I get nervous every time I think about it," Sarah said, setting a hand to her stomach.

"Well, don't," Abby said, even though she wished she could take her own advice. "Want to plan on coming to my place tomorrow and we can walk over together?"

"I'd love that," Sarah said with a grin. "Just think. We can show off our fresh manicures and pedicures."

That was one thing to look forward to. Abby wasn't so sure about the rest. She gave Sarah quick directions to her apartment and then motioned to her bike. "I pedaled over."

"I walked." Sarah hopped down the stairs, turning when she reached the bottom. "See you tomorrow for our big night!"

Abby was trying to not think about it. She'd worry about it tomorrow, she decided. Her old motto, and one that was sometimes good to pull out every once in a while.

The temperature had dropped during the time they'd been inside and Abby shivered as she walked across the sidewalk to her bike. The sun was low in the sky, an orange glow over the horizon that would soon fade into the sea, and the lights twinkled on Main Street. A steady breeze was blowing in off the ocean, and there was a wonderful smell of salt in the air.

Still, it did little to cool the heat that still burned in her face, and the anger that had settled in her chest, like a great big ball of fire that she couldn't snuff out, no matter how badly she wanted to.

Zach was back in Oyster Bay. Turning up everywhere

she went. Once, the thought would have thrilled her. Now…it scared her. This town had been her safe place, her respite, she had grown comfortable in the thought of never having to run into him again, of never having to be reminded. Now that was all there was. Memories. Of another time and place.

"Hey!"

She stopped and closed her eyes. Could this night get any worse?

"Abby, wait up!" He was coming, from behind, she could make out the sound of his heels on the sidewalk, loud and persistent.

She forced herself to turn around, hating the little flutter that arose in her stomach when she saw his face. That handsome face…Even when she saw it every day, even when it felt like it belonged to her, she'd never stopped admiring that face. But now. She didn't want to look at it. She really needed to get away from it.

"Gotta go!" she called as she hurried to steady her bike. She swung one leg over the side and began to pedal.

"Abby!"

He was catching up, closing the distance between them, and this time she didn't waver. She pedaled. Hard and fast and furious, turning onto the nearest side street where storefronts turned to historic homes tucked behind white picket fences.

She pedaled until she wasn't sure her legs would keep up with her anymore and her hair was blowing behind her, until her heart was pumping in her chest and she was grinning from sheer exhilaration, from the speed, from her freedom.

She stood, putting the weight into her feet, eager to put more power into her speed, when the smooth sole of her sandal slipped on the pedal. Her balance shifted to the left, and she gripped the handlebars tighter, but it was no use. She slid off the seat, hovering somewhere over the frame of the bike, the odds of ending this gracefully lower than the odds of being struck by lightning on a warm, sunny day.

Gritting her teeth, she did her best to steer to the patch of grass, hoping for a soft landing, but the curb caught the front tire and then…there was dirt. And pain. And cement.

And probably a fair amount of blood too.

She didn't know what to cry out about harder. That she had crashed her bike and skinned her arm and leg and—well, crap—her skirt was now around her waist and she wasn't wearing her most flattering pair of underwear either. In fact—Oh, *no, no, no, no*. She had the heart-stopping realization that she was wearing the flesh colored ones, seeing that her skirt was light blue and all that. And now…Oh, dear God, she thought heavily. Now said skirt was around her waist, tangled in the gears of the bike, and by all intents and purposes her ass looked…bare.

And Zach. Zach was still behind her. Coming nearer, if the steady tread of his footsteps said anything.

Quickly, she tried to move the bike enough to let her wrestle her skirt down into place, but Zach was already there, lifting it off her, before she'd had the chance.

She locked his eyes for one miserable moment and then, because there was no escaping this in the physical sense, simply closed her eyes and lay back on the grass, wondering if it might have been better if she'd just simply hit a tree instead of a curb, just enough so she wouldn't have to be conscious for this bone-deep humiliation.

He was pulling her to her feet now, his hand so warm and his grip so sure that she really did think she would burst into tears then. But no, no, she had a job to do. She snatched her hand free the moment her feet were steady and began smoothing her skirt, which was now blowing in the wind, and…Nice. He was trying not to laugh.

"I could have killed myself, you know!" She furiously pushed at her skirt and began inspecting herself, realizing with surprise that the only cut was a scuff to the right knee. Her elbow was burning, no doubt from being dragged with full body weight over the grass, and she cupped it unhappily. Damn him. If he'd never come back, she would have been happily pulling into her apartment's courtyard right now, her bike as intact as her pride.

But he was here, and he wasn't laughing, well, only a little, and only, in fairness, when he'd realized that she wasn't bleeding. Or dying. Not in the physical sense at least.

"That eager to get away from me, eh?"

Oh, and there it was. The little part of her that melted

every time he looked at her that way, his eyes searching, his brow a little crinkled, his smile slightly slipped but still hopeful.

"Yes," she said, stiffening.

"Hey." His voice was gentle, low, and damn it if it wasn't wholly sincere. "I'm sorry about that back there. I was..."

Jealous. He'd been jealous. And she'd been way too happy to know that he was. And where did that leave either of them?

"Can I make it up to you?" He thrust his hands in his pockets and looked at her. "Buy you an ice cream?"

"Ice cream?" She should say no. That she was hurt, inside and out, that she needed to go home, to her safe place, her cozy little five-hundred-square-foot, sunlight-filled box that he'd never touched, that didn't fill her with a single memory.

Instead, she said, "I do like ice cream."

His grin was lopsided, and she could tell that he was pleased. Without asking, he took her bike by the handlebars and started wheeling it back in the direction of town, walking slowly enough so that she could limp along beside him without too much effort.

"You know, you really should wear a helmet," he scolded her.

"Why, Zach," she teased, desperate to lighten the mood. "I didn't know you cared."

"I've always cared," he said, glancing sidelong at her.

And for a moment, she almost dared to believe it was true. But then she flashed back to that day when her world crashed down and her heart felt like it was breaking into a thousand pieces, and how she hovered outside his apartment building, wondering if he'd change his mind. But he hadn't.

She swallowed hard and he looked away. They walked in silence for a while, until they had turned back onto Main and the lights from the ice cream parlor came into view. It was one of her favorite places in town—an old establishment that, like many of the local businesses, had been passed down through generations. Now owned and operated by Francesca Johnson, a former classmate of Abby's, and great-granddaughter of the founder, it had undergone a subtle face-lift in the past two years, but the recipes never changed.

Sometimes things didn't, after all. Even, Abby thought, when she wanted them to.

Zach parked her biked against a bench and they walked around back to the order window, bypassing the line inside and the crowded wrought iron café tables filled with toddlers and tired mothers and young couples out on a date.

"Two chocolate cones," Zach told the teenage girl working the window and then, as if suddenly catching himself, he turned to Abby, his expression guilty. "Unless…You always liked chocolate."

She smiled. She owed him that much, she supposed. "I still like chocolate."

"Glad to know that some things about you are the same."

"What's that supposed to mean?" Abby asked as she took her cone from the girl and licked the bottom, before it dripped all over her hand.

Zach stuffed a couple bucks in the tip jar and led them toward the edge of the patio. It was a dark corner, and secluded, but Abby didn't want to sit. Fortunately, Zach didn't want to either.

He tipped his head toward the beach, and she nodded. Even growing up here, she never tired of the feeling of sand between her toes, or the sound of waves lapping at the shore. It centered her. Calmed her. And tonight, she needed those powers more than ever.

"You're different than you were back in college."

"That was a long time ago," she reminded him, as she toed off her sandals. She bent to pick them up, careful not to tip her cone. The sand was cool beneath her feet, reassuring. She forced herself to take another lick from her ice cream. She didn't like thinking about that time in her life. Her parents dying. All those trips back and forth from Oyster Bay to college until college finally ended and she could get back to where she was needed, and needed to be. Zach breaking up with her. Her life wide open and lacking direction, all plans gone.

When she'd first started college she'd been studying marketing, but then her world tipped, and she was lost, and she was grasping, and she was switching majors and losing focus and the only constant, the only thing she could rely on, was Zach. Until she couldn't.

"But you're not completely different. You still have that fire in you. That spark." He hesitated for a moment. "It was what made me first fall in love with you."

He gave her a bashful grin and she stiffened, not quite sure how to reply and happy that the farther they ventured from the lights of Main Street, the less likely he was to make out the heat that reddened her face.

She considered giving a compliment in return, that he was still as driven as ever. But was that even true? He was back in Oyster Bay, working at the local paper. She couldn't make any sense of it.

"Why'd you come back to town?" she asked, looking at him properly.

He took his time replying, focusing on his feet and the sand beneath them. "I was ready for a change, I suppose."

"And working at the paper. That's what you plan to do?"

"In between planning festivals," he said with a grin.

Abby blew out a sigh of frustration. He was being evasive, and she didn't like it. But then, she supposed she'd lost dibs on the truth years ago. He didn't need to share with her. She wasn't a part of his life anymore.

Except that lately, this past week, she'd felt like she was.

*

Zach looked up at the moon. It was full tonight, lighting up the sky and casting shadows over Abby's face. He tried to think of something to say, something that would lighten the mood and shift the topic away from him, but he failed.

Did Abby really have an interest in Brad of all people? Back in school, he was the class clown; surely she remembered his stunts. And what about the time he and his brothers had toilet-papered Dottie Joyce's house? Sure, she was a ripe pain in the butt most of the time, but that was taking it too far.

And what if she did have an interest in Brad? There was nothing he could do to stop her. He'd had his chance, back when she'd been his. He could have asked her to marry him. He'd thought about it, but maybe not often enough. He'd assumed that she'd go along with his plan, follow him where he went, that they'd travel the world together. What he hadn't expected was for Abby to buckle down, to want to come back to this sleepy place.

Any more than he expected to end up back here one day himself.

"Abby, there's something I need to say," he said, stopping right where the water met the sand. His shoes were going to get wet if he kept going, and he should have stopped to take them off, but he was out of the habit.

She looked alarmed, her face aglow in the cold

moonlight, and she took the last few bites of her ice cream, watching him.

"I'm sorry, Abby," he said. There. He'd said it.

Her eyes narrowed a bit. "Sorry for what?"

"For hurting you," he said, feeling the relief roll off his shoulders with the words. He'd tried to tell her, but now he had to try to make her see. "I thought I was doing what was best for you, what you wanted."

"Wait." She dipped her chin and shifted her weight on her feet until she was looking him square in the eye. "Are you talking about when you dumped me?"

"I didn't dump you." He pulled in a sigh. Ran a hand through his hair. "Jesus, Abby, I did what I thought you wanted!"

"What I wanted?" she repeated. "What I wanted was *you*, Zach."

The words tore right through him, sharp as any knife, and any doubt that he'd made a terrible mistake was erased. "You wanted to come back to Oyster Bay," he reminded her. In his career he'd learned to focus on the facts, to try to take his emotions out of a situation. He'd failed at it every time, just like he was failing now.

"You used that as your excuse," she said.

He shook his head. "No. It wasn't an excuse. You'd been through a lot. You needed your family."

"I needed you," she insisted.

He closed his eyes. This wasn't how he thought it would go. He thought she would hear him out, once and for all, that she'd argue, or understand. Either was better than this...this reminder of his choice. Of what it cost him. Of what he'd once been to her.

"No," he said firmly, remembering all too well the words she had said to him back then. "You said you needed them. That you couldn't come with me, didn't want to come with me, because you wanted to be here, in Oyster Bay, with your grandmother and your sisters. Bridget was a single mother with a baby, your grandmother was all alone in that big house, and you thought they needed you. You wanted to come back here!"

"Why is that such a terrible thing?" she asked, hurt in her voice.

"It's not a terrible thing," he said. And it was something he understood now more than he could have back then. "It's a wonderful thing. But it wasn't what I wanted for myself."

She shook her head and looked away, out toward the ocean, as if searching for something in the waves. He understood. He'd do the same if he could. Look for a way back, a way to understand then what he knew now. Jobs came and went, but people didn't. Not if you held on.

But then, even when you did they sometimes slipped away, he thought, looking at Abby.

"You'd been through so much," he said. "Your parents...Who was I to stop you from going home to your family?"

"You could have come with me," she said, her voice

so soft it was nearly lost in the breeze.

She looked at him, sidelong, and the hurt in her eyes matched the pain in his chest, and just for one moment, he dared to think she got it. She understood. Her heart broke that day. But his heart broke too.

"You know I couldn't have," he said. "You know I wouldn't have been happy."

Her mouth pinched. He'd lost her again. That connection was so fleeting. "I didn't make you happy enough."

"We didn't make each other happy enough for everything we would have had to give up. Is that what you wanted, Abby? For me to come back to Oyster Bay, work for the local paper, throw aside everything that I'd worked for?" He knew it wasn't what she wanted for him. It wasn't what he'd wanted for himself. And yet here he was. "I would have resented you back then. Just like you would have resented me if you'd come with me."

"Is that what you tell yourself?" Her tone was sarcastic, bitter even.

"It is, actually." Because it was the truth, damn it.

There was a long silence before she spoke again. "But you're back now. So why now? Why not then?"

It was a fair question, but one he didn't know the answer to. Not really. "We've changed, Abby. We grew up." He shrugged. "You did what you wanted. You came back. I did what I wanted. I didn't. But...I never stopped thinking of you."

"Well, I didn't think of you," she said, blinking quickly.

Tears shone in her eyes, and hurt burned so strong it took everything in him not to reach out and grab her, to hold her close, sink his face into her hair, breathe her smell. "I couldn't...think of you."

It hurt. It hurt bad. But he understood.

"You moved on," he said, nodding his head.

"Yes. No." She laughed, but she wasn't amused. "I tried to."

"Abby." He reached out a hand, stretched it out, until his fingers grazed hers. He waited to see if she would snatch back, run off, grab her bike and pedal it all the way home, not falling this time. But she just looked at him, with tears in her eyes and an understanding that only the two of them could share.

He stepped forward, knowing that he had to try, and that he couldn't resist, even if she rejected him. Her hair was blowing in the wind, whipping across her face now, and he brushed it back. One tear slipped from her eye and trailed its way down her cheek. She looked down, her eyelashes wet, and sighed.

"Zach."

But that was all she needed to say. That sweet voice. That sweet girl she once was. The girl who would make him laugh. The girl who had made him cry.

He leaned into her, setting one hand carefully on her waist, holding his breath for the moment when their lips would touch and all this...stuff...would be behind them.

But all at once he felt her body stiffen, and her chin

snapped upright, and she was backing away, farther and farther until she turned, without a word, and ran, all the way back to the ice cream shop, until nothing was left of her but her footprints in the sand.

Chapter Nine

The next night, at seven sharp, Sarah rang Abby's doorbell. Abby grabbed her handbag, opened the door, and immediately knew that they were going to have to be fashionably late. Not that she particularly minded. She'd been dreading this night ever since Sarah first broached the idea, and even more so today, when she thought of how she'd left things off with Zach last night.

Would he just pretend it hadn't happened? That he hadn't tried to kiss her and that she hadn't run off? Or would he say something, want to talk it out?

Shove it under the bed, that was what she hoped to do. But then, that was how she used to live her life, head in the sand, trying not to think about things she didn't want to think about, never looking back, but never moving forward either. That couldn't go on indefinitely, and she didn't want it to. Now that she had a taste of what it felt like to take a chance again, to strive for something, well, she had to keep going.

And tonight just might be the night she could at least get Zach to turn things around for her career and write a damn retraction.

She doubted that the famous Zachary Dillon had ever been forced to print a retraction in his life! Of course, the *Oyster Bay Gazette* was known for them. There was the time that Estelle Hancock's eyes were described as green instead of hazel, a feature she was most proud of, and she'd demanded an accurate correction, after marching down to the office and pulling off her glasses, so everyone had a clear look of the flecks of brown around her pupils. And then there was the time that a reporter had mistakenly referred to the mayor's wife as Nasty instead of Nancy—a Freudian slip if ever there was one.

So really, would it kill Zach to go back on his word? Or did he still hold the same opinion? Still want to stick to it? Did his career still matter that much?

"Come on in," Abby said, setting her bag down on the small bench that separated her front hall space from her living and kitchen combo. She slipped off her sandals, relaxing already.

"But we'll be late!" Sarah looked alarmed.

Abby pulled her inside and closed the door behind her, tsking as she gave her friend the full once-over. And here she thought Bridget was hopeless! What, with her mom jeans that were a solid fifteen years out of style, and her linen button-down shirts that were easily unisex. Most of the time, she looked like a middle-aged wife, not a single woman in her prime. For years, she had tried to encourage Bridget to dress in a more appealing way, unhook an extra button, add a touch of blush, but each time Bridget had shooed her off, claiming she wasn't looking to date again. It took everything in Abby not to tell her that, believe it or not, she understood, but her way of handling life had always been different than her oldest sister's. While Bridget was content sitting at home with a romance novel to fill her lonely nights, Abby preferred to get out, distract herself, not focus on what she'd lost. So while she was dating Charlie and Chase and Rob and Brian, Bridget was sitting home alone, perfectly content in her flannel pajamas. Until Jack came along... The problem was that Jack seemed to love Bridget as she was, frumpy clothes and all. Sure, this was a good thing, to be loved as you were, but would it kill Bridget to take her hair out of that ponytail for once?

Unlike Bridget, Sarah was on the prowl and she wasn't shy in admitting this. Yet, she was dressed as if she were on her way to visit her grandmother instead. "Is this how you dressed for your online dates?"

Sarah looked down at her outfit—chinos in an indeterminable shade of beige, a white tank top that Abby could certainly work with, and, the linchpin, a light blue cardigan that she'd buttoned halfway up and which hung loosely at her hips. A pair of ballet flats technically completed the look.

"Not in the winter," she said. "For my winter dates, I liked to wear jeans and a black turtleneck—"

Abby held up a hand as her eyes closed. She'd heard enough.

"Come into my bedroom," she said, leading the way to the only other room in the apartment, other than the bathroom. The apartment was small, with an open floor plan, but Abby loved it. She'd lived here for years, long before Mimi had gone to Serenity Hills, even if she did have some guilt over that. If she'd still been home, she would have noticed things like Mimi taking the kettle off the stove and failing to turn off the burner for a few hours...

Bridget insisted that there was nothing Abby could have done long term. Mimi needed round the clock care. It was best for her, given her age.

And maybe it was... After all, now Mimi was getting married to a man from the nursing home, and Bridget was able to buy back their house and turn it into a thriving business.

Everything had worked out for them. But would it work out for her?

Her stomach felt funny every time she thought of that review and the cancellation for the weekend. Would there be another next week?

Abby hadn't worked up the courage to tell Bridget about the food truck at the festival yet. This morning

Bridget had been too busy running out to the back porch every five minutes, seeing as the humidity had tapered and everyone wanted to enjoy the sunshine with their eggs. But tomorrow...tomorrow she'd have to tell her. Or maybe she'd wait. Yes, waiting would be best. She'd figure out her plan. Then she'd share it, only once she knew it would be a success.

And it had to be a success, Abby thought, bringing her thumb to her mouth and then quickly setting it back again before she chewed off a freshly manicured nail.

"Oh, no." Sarah studied her face with a worried stitch between her brow. "Is it really that bad?"

"Well, it's certainly more in the range of *work* attire, but I can work with the tank top." Abby led Sarah over to her closet, wishing that it wasn't such a mess. It was a good thing her sisters seldom stopped by. Bridget would cluck her tongue and Margo would want to color coordinate everything and then start talking about updating the furniture. Abby had already been advised on the benefits of a "statement" piece. She liked to think that her velvet green couch she'd picked up secondhand when she first took over the lease was her statement piece, but what did she know? That was Margo's territory, and cooking and baking were hers.

Abby began rifling through some options. She didn't purchase many clothes; she preferred to spend her money on cookbooks and food for new recipes, but what she had she took care of, well, aside from the heap that seemed to grow forever higher over in the corner behind her door…

"How about this skirt?" She held up a chambray knee-length skirt triumphantly. She'd bought it over the winter on a rare shopping trip with her sisters. It was from last season and marked down so low that she couldn't resist, even if she was supposed to be looking for something for Mimi's birthday… "With the white top and some fun jewelry, it will be perfect."

Sarah tugged at her cardigan. "I don't know."

"Nuns wear cardigans," Abby told her firmly. "And the ladies in Serenity Hills."

Sarah laughed. "True. But…what if I get cold?"

"Then you can ask Brad to keep you warm," Abby replied with a wink.

Sarah lit up like a Christmas tree. As she unbuttoned her sweater, she said, "Thanks for doing this for me, Abby. You're a good person, and I have a feeling that by end of tonight, Zach is going to be wondering why the two of you ever split up."

"Oh, he knows why," Abby said, taking the sweater from Sarah and tossing it on her bed.

"Did you break his heart?" Sarah asked wistfully as she tried to hide behind the closet door to change. Clearly, she hadn't grown up with two sisters.

"More like the other way around," Abby said with a snort.

"That's not what he said," Sarah said.

Startled, Abby all but pushed the closet door closed to look her friend in the eye. "He said that? What did he say?" And better yet, why did she care?

"He said that you dated in college and it didn't work out and that he'd always been sad about that."

Yes, so he'd said. He'd gone his way, she'd gone hers. And while he seemed to have regrets, it didn't change anything.

Abby thought about that for a few seconds. "Well, his choice."

Just like it had been his choice to almost kiss her last night. And her choice not to let him.

Pensively, she walked over to her dresser and began rifling through the jewelry box she'd added to over the years. It was just costume jewelry, and none of it really matched, but she loved each and every piece, especially the chunky necklace with the hot pink rhinestones.

She held it up to her neck and looked at herself in the mirror.

"You have to put that on," Sarah said, answering Abby's own thoughts.

"I don't want to look like I care," Abby said, setting it back. Her jeans and a simple light pink tank were appropriate but hardly compelling, and she'd wanted it that way.

"But why shouldn't you?" Sarah asked. "Don't you want him to see what he's been missing?"

I missed you. Abby closed her eyes as his voice filled her head.

"You know what, Sarah? You're right." Abby pulled the necklace from the box and slid it around her neck. It glittered against her collarbone and gave her a strange sense of excitement and possibility.

Sarah came up beside her and admired herself in the mirror. The tank top and skirt made her look youthful and flirty. "Have to say that you were right, too. Now, mind if I borrow a necklace?"

Abby grinned. "I know just the one."

*

As soon as they arrived at Dunley's, Abby felt sick with nerves. She looked at Sarah, who, from the green hue that had taken over her face, seemed even worse off, if such a thing were possible.

What was she supposed to say when she walked in? Oh, hey, Zach, sorry that I ran off on you twice last night, but seeing as you ran off on me when we were supposed to be in love, maybe we can call it even?

She looked down at her leg, which still felt tender from her fall off the bike. She hadn't mentioned that to Sarah yet, and she doubted she would. The only thing that would have made the situation more humiliating was if a dog had come along and lifted his leg to the grass in which she was sprawled.

"It's not too late to turn back," she suddenly said, feeling desperate. "Bottle of white, a pizza from DiSotto's, and a marathon of trash TV?" Abby waggled her eyebrows, hoping that Sarah would just chicken out and give her the excuse she needed to go home and, well, pull a Bridget. Minus the romance novel. A good murder mystery would suit her better.

"I can't turn back now." Sarah blew out a shaky breath. "I couldn't eat all day from nerves, and if we don't go in tonight, I may never work up the courage again."

"Sounds like another basket of scones is in order for tomorrow," Abby said, not that she was so sure she wanted to make another stop at the *Gazette*.

"And Brad is so cute. Before long he could have another girlfriend!"

Abby didn't have the heart to correct her. Every girl in town grew up with Brad and knew his childhood antics. But hey, if Sarah wanted to think that Brad's availability was as fleeting as a beachfront cottage in August, who was she to argue? "Well, let's do this then."

She reached for the door handle, the air-conditioning hitting her in a sudden rush. God, her stomach just dropped, and she didn't think it could do that anymore. It hadn't, not really, not for Chase or the male nurse or half the other guys that she eyed across the room or dated over the years. Not when she was brutally honest with herself, which was something she'd tried to avoid being, because…well, it was just easier that way.

The only man she'd ever been invested in was sitting at the bar, in a cool blue linen shirt rolled at the arms. He caught her eye at once and Brad swiveled around on his chair and she suddenly remembered that Brad had a crush on Margo years before she met Eddie. A thing for older ladies.. Not that she'd be telling Sarah as much. Instead she would highlight that Brad was captain of the basketball team. She also wouldn't bring up that he couldn't pass Spanish two years in a row. After all, who was she to judge? Maybe he just enjoyed the class too much to give it up. Maybe it had been good for his game to shoot those balls of paper into the poor teacher's sombrero ...Tonight was a big night for Sarah. Best to stay positive.

Speaking of... Abby whipped around, searching for her friend, who'd apparently vanished into thin air.

"She went into the ladies," Zach answered for her.

"Oh." Well, fabulous. Just her, then. And Zach. And that look. Oh, and Brad, of course. The man he thought she was supposedly interested in. She'd forgotten about that part. Darn it.

From the tightness in Zach's jaw, he hadn't.

"Should we get a table?" she asked, for lack of anything else to contribute just now. This was awkward, really awkward, and even Brad looked a little confused as to why he was here.

Zach grinned as he slid off his chair and beat Brad to the front of the line, where he followed her, closely, too closely really, as she shifted around the room, eyeing the door. He'd almost kissed her, he really had, and with a horrible, sickening, gut-wrenching realization, she suddenly knew that a small part of her wanted him to try again.

Nonsense! With purpose, she walked to the only open table in sight. A booth, as luck would have it, in the back corner of the room, where the band usually set up around eight and where conversation would be difficult.

She calculated the arrangement as she walked. The girls on one side and the guys on the other was the only way to get out of sitting right next to Zach all night. But that might make it a bit hard for Sarah to talk to Brad, and that really was the purpose of the evening after all.

Brad slid into one side of the booth and Zach eyed her, as if challenging her to pick a side, then and there. With great reluctance, she slid into the empty booth just as Sarah reappeared, flush faced and starry eyed.

Abby couldn't look at Zach when she said, "You slide in with Brad, Sarah." God knew that if left to her own devices, she'd have done no such thing.

Fighting off a smile, Zach was left to slide in next to her, and he did so, close enough that their thighs skimmed and a surge of heat shot through her stomach. She scooted to the left, and God help her, he did too.

She flashed him a look, but he still didn't budge. Instead, he pulled out the menu and pretended to be wholly engrossed, oblivious to the fact that his body was now pressing up against her and that she could feel his heat, smell that soap that lingered deep in the fibers of his shirt and would no doubt rub off on hers.

Now she'd have to do laundry this weekend.

"Should we get some appetizers?"

It was just supposed to be drinks, and Abby had secretly hoped it would be an hour at best. An hour of torture and suffering and doing her best to ignore the feelings that were brewing inside her. But then she remembered that Sarah hadn't eaten for a day and that she'd no doubt be drinking. "Yes," Abby said firmly, opening her own menu. "Ryan does a great spinach dip."

Actually, it wasn't quite as good as her own spinach dip, but there was no need to mention that. She'd honed and perfected that recipe for years, and it was a staple when she was invited to things like New Year's parties or, lately, baby or bridal showers.

While everyone else was oohing and awing over pink fuzzy blankets or sexy lingerie, Abby usually sat to the side, carefully trying each item on her plate, analyzing it for taste and improvement.

Sometimes she got a new idea, like the time Caitie Martin invited all the girls from high school over for her engagement shower, which was really a chance to show off her new house, and her new engagement ring, and a clever way to disguise the fact that she was marrying Mike Wallace, who was a notorious nose picker all the way up through grade nine, and she couldn't be foolish enough to think they'd all forgotten that.

Caitie liked to cook, and she was all too happy to show them all the gadgets she'd registered for and already put to use. Abby had questioned whether this might be jinxing things a bit, considering she wasn't scheduled to walk down the aisle for another six months, but she said nothing and smiled politely along with all the other girls, and yes, there was a twinge of envy, but not for the two-carat diamond or the upcoming honeymoon in Paris, but oh, she envied that KitchenAid mixer, something every single cook on television had and something she really couldn't afford to buy for herself, unless she didn't care about keeping the lights on next month.

She made a silent promise to herself to buy that mixer for her thirtieth birthday. Well, actually she had considered hinting to Bridget that they needed one for the inn, but seeing as she wasn't exactly on steady ground, now probably wasn't the best time to be calling in favors.

With the orders placed, silence fell around the table. Sarah glanced nervously at Brad. Zach seemed to almost glare at Brad. And Brad just sat there, oblivious.

Abby sighed. She was so used to Margo being the peacemaker in her family since her return to town last fall, but it seemed tonight it was her night to take charge.

"Haven't seen you around much, Brad," she said, which wasn't exactly true. Brad lived just down the street from her and he was often out walking his golden retriever, Buddy. "Things busy at the paper?"

"Busy enough," he said with a shrug.

"You write the sports column, right?" Not that she read it, but she'd done her research, eliminating possibilities for the mystery reviewer.

"Yeah, I'm lucky."

"They don't ever, say, assign you to a different topic? Reviewing restaurants, that type of thing?" Abby glanced sidelong at Zach, to see if he'd squirm.

"Nah," Brad said. "Sports are kind of my thing."

Abby nodded. "Sarah, did you know Brad was captain of the basketball team in high school?"

"Wow," Sarah said, blushing a little.

Brad gave a modest grin. "I was okay."

"Better than okay," Abby said, trying to send Sarah a message with her eyes across the table. Beside her she felt Zach stiffen.

"I bet you were pretty good to be captain," Sarah said, and Abby felt an inner glow. The pupil was learning. This might just work out after all.

"Well, I took a few good shots in my day," Brad said a little humbly, and Abby found herself softening toward him. He was hardly the same punk kid. He'd grown up, lost the ego, seemed downright nice, really.

"You're too modest. You were voted MVP three seasons from what I recall!" Abby could practically feel Zach's lip curl, but she didn't feed into it. She was here to help Sarah. If Zach wanted to get jealous in the meantime, well, who was she to stop him?

"What does it take to earn that?" Sarah asked, seeming to be feeling more relaxed by the minute. And their drinks hadn't even arrived yet!

As she and Brad started chatting about how he might consider coaching for the high school team next fall,

Zach elbowed her and said, "Hate to break it to you, but I think Brad might have a thing for Sarah."

As nice as it would be to punish Zach a bit longer, she decided to cut him a break. "That was the plan all along."

His mouth pulled into a lopsided grin, and for one horrible moment she thought he might mention the kiss, or the almost kiss, or…whatever it was.

Their drinks arrived then, and she was grateful for the disruption. She sipped her wine, deciding to pass on the appetizers when they quickly followed. She wasn't hungry. Her stomach was too fluttery. Besides, she'd eaten just about everything that was on the menu here. There was nothing to taste test.

"Have you decided what to make for the festival?" Zach asked.

So they were keeping it neutral. She wasn't sure why she was so disappointed by this.

"I was thinking my blueberry scones," she said, watching him carefully. Sure enough, he reached for his beer and took a long sip, avoiding eye contract. Oh, enough! She turned so that her back was against the wall and she was properly facing him on the bench. "Why don't you just come out and admit that you wrote that review."

"Those reviews are supposed to be anonymous," Zach replied calmly.

"Drop the act, Zach, I saw you at the inn that day, and only five of the scones in that batch went out, and one was on your plate."

"And what if I did write it?" he asked.

He had her there. She hadn't thought it out much further.

"Then I'd ask you to write a retraction," she said, growing angry.

"Retraction?" His expression was a mix of surprise and amusement. "I've never had to print a retraction in my entire career!"

"Then let me be the first," she said, staring him down. He couldn't seriously object to setting the record straight, explaining that the food was, in fact, delicious. Surely everyone was allowed one bad day!

"I don't think you understand how that looks for a journalist's career," he said gravely.

The blood was boiling within her now and she eyed her glass of wine, having to fight the urge to pick it up and fling its contents. "What about my career?"

"Hey, now, what's going on?" Brad asked, growing aware of the conversation. Beside him, Sarah's eyes were wide with concern.

"Zach seems to be under the false impression that his career is more important than mine," Abby said. Just like he'd thought his choices and preferences were more important all those years ago. It had never changed. Still. It was all about his work. His career. What suited him best.

"I've got this, Brad," Zach said, holding up a hand, and Brad looking relieved to resume more lighthearted conversation with the once again beaming Sarah.

Abby was starting to feel like a caged animal, pressed against the wall of the booth, Zach blocking her exit. And maybe he preferred it that way. Maybe he'd staged it.

"You know I wrote that article," he said in such a low voice that she almost didn't hear him.

Her hearted started to pound. "Excuse me?" She needed clarification. She needed this crystal clear. Actually, she needed it shouted from the bar. His confession.

"I wrote the article before I knew that you had made the scones," he said, looking at her sheepishly.

Abby didn't see how this could make her feel any better. He hadn't liked the scones. Hadn't liked the food she'd served in general. And that hurt. It hurt a hell of a lot more than the review itself.

"So you're saying that if you had known I made them, you would have said something else?"

"Yes," he said flatly, and she knew he was telling the truth.

"So, you would have lied," she said, considering this. "And as a journalist, don't you have your reputation to live up to?"

Zach sighed. "Abby, I'm sorry. Believe me when I say that the last thing I wanted to do was upset you or hurt your job."

Job. Nice. So much for being respected for what she did. So much for her life choices and passions mattering to him.

"Well, it's a family business," she replied.

"And you weren't exactly nice to me that morning," he shot back.

"So you took it out on my family's business?"

"I wrote an honest review," he said. "There were some nice things in there too, if you bothered to read the whole thing."

"And you won't print a retraction?"

"Abby," he said wearily. "It's too late to print a retraction. That article came out almost two weeks ago."

"And you chose not to write a retraction even though you knew by the day it came out that I was the cook at the inn," she clarified, maybe a little too loudly. She glanced at Brad and Sarah, who were now inching out of the booth, Brad muttering something about catching a seat at the bar so they could hear each other better, the band starting soon and all. Nice, polite excuse. Yep, solid, good, honest guy. Abby gave Sarah her stamp of approval on that one.

On Zach, though… She shook her head. Nothing had changed. His career trumped all else. Why did she think it would suddenly be different?

"I'm sorry, Abby. As soon as I knew you were the cook there, I knew I'd made a big mistake. If I could turn back time, I would."

She hesitated, thinking of everything he'd said last night, and everything he'd said just now, and none of it made her feel any better. "But you can't," she said, suddenly feeling very, very depressed. "I need to go. I'm tired."

"Are you sure?" he said, but he was inching away, giving her space, and somehow this small gesture was enough to make her want to stay, enough to make her want to forgive and to believe that things could be different. But she just couldn't.

"I'm sure," she said sadly as she slid out and began walking to the door, without looking back. Sure that he'd hurt her. Sure that he was probably sorry. And sure that as much as she hated to admit it, a part of her still loved him. A part of her still cared.

*

"You're home early," Melanie accused from the comfort of her recliner. A new purchase, she'd informed Zach rather proudly when he'd stared at it in disbelief upon his arrival. It was nearly identical to the one their grandfather had lived in from the moment he retired up until the day he died. No one was allowed to sit in that chair. But now Melanie had one of her very own. And, like good old Gramps, she was content to park herself in it for long periods of time.

He was dismayed to see that she was sitting in the exact position she'd been in when he left her a couple of hours ago, only the bowl of pretzels was now just a bowl of crumbs, and the box of wine ("It's good!" she'd enthused when he'd pointed to it in the fridge, skeptical) was out on the counter.

"There's some left," she said, noticing him eyeing it. "I'm telling you. It's good."

Oh, what the hell? It had been a rough day. A rough week. Seeing as he hadn't thought to pick up any beer, his options were this or water.

He took a juice glass from the top shelf and poured it to the rim, almost afraid to take a sip. When in Rome, he thought, bringing it to his lips.

Melanie was watching him carefully, waiting for his response.

He smacked his lips. "Not bad," he admitted, amused.

She grinned. "Told you so."

He grinned back. He hadn't heard her say that since they were kids, and he suddenly felt a wave of nostalgia for those days. Back then, he and Melanie had been close, or at least as close as brothers and sisters went. They rarely fought, got along well, always seemed to have each other's back.

He wanted to get back to that again.

"You could have come out with us tonight," he said, as he came around to sit on the couch, which was doubling as his bed these days. He'd have to change that, once he'd figured things out. "Still mad at me for getting you roped into volunteering for the festival?"

Melanie sighed. "You know Mom doesn't back down once she has an idea. Knowing her, she would have signed me up for something even if I hadn't attended the meeting."

"Is it so bad?" He had to agree with his mother that Melanie could use a reason to put on some real clothes and leave the house on evenings and weekends.

"You don't understand," Melanie said, looking annoyed when she glanced back at the television screen and saw that the commercial break was over.

"Try me," he said, leaning back on a throw pillow. Melanie's apartment was full of them. They were on her bed, on the couch, one was even on her lap now. He could stick to the easy questions and inquire about this instead, but decided to leave it for another day.

"You went away. You had experiences. Coming back here…it's like another of your adventures."

He considered this for a moment, sipping his wine, which he had to admit went down quite easily. Coming back to Oyster Bay was an adventure in some ways, but it was hardly as black and white as Melanie made it out to be.

But thankfully, they weren't talking about him tonight.

"I've never left," she continued. "And before you say anything, I know that was my choice, and I love this town, but sometimes…it's stifling."

He thought about Dottie and the comment she had made at the planning meeting. No doubt whatever was going on in Melanie's life was already part of the gossip mill. It hadn't reached the paper yet, so he had to assume it wasn't so bad.

"When something good happens to you, the whole town knows. When something bad happens, the whole town knows. It's like you can't get a break!"

He looked at her, her face free of makeup, her glasses sliding down her nose, hair in a messy knot on top of her head. Still wearing the same pajamas she'd been in that morning, since Chloe covered the shop every other Saturday. His sister was depressed. He got it. He'd been there.

"I don't judge," he said. "And I also don't know what happened that has you so upset."

She frowned at him. "You mean Mom didn't tell you?"

He shook his head. "Nope." His mother was too busy asking to fold his laundry, offering to help him find an apartment, or better yet, encouraging him to move back into his old room. When he'd announced he had a job at the *Gazette*, he swore she was crying on the phone. He didn't have the heart to tell her it was a temporary position. They needed someone with experience. He needed something to keep him busy and fill the gap on his resume.

Melanie sighed, then looked him square in the eye. "Do you remember Doug McKinney?"

The name was familiar, but he struggled to place it.

"You know," she pressed. "My grade, brown hair, used to date Stephanie Thompson?"

Stephanie Sunshine! That's what they called her. She was always smiling. Even when something bad happened, she had a knee-jerk reaction to laugh or giggle instead of cry. "What ever happened to her?"

Melanie brushed a hand through the air. "Moved to Portland. Has three kids and a white picket fence, last I heard. Probably smiled through every painful contraction."

They laughed, and it felt good, damn good, he thought. Like old times.

"I remember Doug." He cocked an eyebrow, feeling immediately alarmed at the thought of anyone hurting his sister. "What did he do?"

"Dumped me on Valentine's Day, that's what he did." She reached for her wineglass, and, seeming surprised to find it was empty, motioned to his. "Do you mind? There's none left in the box now, I'm assuming."

"It's all yours," he said, passing her his glass, which she drank straight from rather than transferring to her own. They were related, after all.

"How long were you guys together?" he asked, surprised that his mother had never mentioned the relationship when he checked in. Although he didn't check in often, he thought, feeling a little guilty. His days passed too quickly. There was always another story to chase, another interview to set up, another story to write.

"Not long. And that's not the point. It's not that he dumped me. Well, I mean, that *did* suck." She looked at him, giving the same eyebrow lift he'd just given her. "But it's just…so frustrating! I go on dates. I date. And then it ends. And then I go to the shop and hear about everyone else's wonderful and exciting plans. Everyone else is getting married or getting on with their lives!"

"And you're sitting in a recliner chair day after day watching soaps," he finished for her. "You know you won't solve your problems that way."

"No," she said after a pause. "But I can escape them."

She had him there. After all, wasn't that what he was doing here in Oyster Bay?

Chapter Ten

The following Saturday, Abby stood side by side with her sisters in the storefront of Bayside Brides, thinking that she almost would have preferred another cancellation at the inn to wearing the bridesmaid dresses Mimi had chosen.

But there had been no cancellation this weekend, and no mention of the review from Bridget, and so Abby stood here, in a heavy satin ball gown-style dress, in a color that could only be described as avocado.

"Mimi," Margo pleaded. Abby could see the strain in her face, the willpower it was taking to hold back. She was a designer, after all. Color was her thing. "Shouldn't we go with something a little bit more…breezy? What about this beautiful blue chiffon?" She crossed the room, the bustle on her dress making her tread slower than usual.

Abby shot a look at Bridget. For the first time in weeks, she felt a connection with her oldest sister again, a feeling that they really were on the same side.

"Blue?" Mimi didn't look convinced. "Boys wear blue."

"Oh, no, blue is very popular!" Melanie Dillon chimed in, from where she stood, rather tensely, near the counter. She'd started whispering her apologies the moment she distributed the dresses, and much as Abby would have liked to place blame, this wasn't Melanie's fault any more than her brother's selfish behavior was.

"You know the saying, something borrowed, something blue!" Margo's eyes looked a little wild as she held up the chic dress in a beautiful shade of aquamarine. It was a dramatic contrast to the one she was wearing. And despite both Margo and Abby having auburn hair, for once, green was failing them. This particular shade made Margo's skin look pasty, and her face seemed drained of color.

Maybe that was the fear. Fear of walking down the aisle in this getup.

"Or a lovely pink!" Margo tried.

"Oh, we have some *lovely* pinks," Melanie said, nodding quickly as she rushed over to a wall of pink gowns and began rifling through them.

Now it was Bridget's turn to hurry across the room, the heavy fabric making a swooshing sound as she did. "You know that pink is Emma's absolute *favorite* color,

Mimi."

Ah, the kid card. No one ever wanted to disappoint Emma. A smart move. Well played, Abby thought, feeling hopeful.

But Mimi just pinched her lips and said, "Pink is overused. Besides, it won't look good with Abby's red hair."

"Red?" Abby met her two sister's wide eyes as she brought a hand to her head. "My hair is a dark chestnut, Mimi."

"If that's what they're calling it these days." Mimi pinched her lips a little tighter and set her hands in her lap with a huff.

Melanie took that moment to disappear, claiming she heard the phone ringing in the stock room. Abby turned to the three-way mirror, trying to keep her gaze from drifting down to the large green mess of a dress, and studied her hair. It was the same as Margo's. It was decidedly auburn and she was not having an Anne Shirley moment.

She glanced at Margo, who flashed her a warning look, and despite her growing temper, Abby kept her mouth shut. They had to pick their battles, and right now the priority was finding a more suitable bridesmaid dress.

"And what about Emma?" Bridget pleaded. She would play that card to the bitter end if she was smart. "She had her little heart set on pink, Mimi! You wouldn't want to let her down…"

Mimi seemed to consider this for a moment. "Fine then."

The girls all smiled in relief, and, like magic, Melanie reappeared, smiling broadly. "Ah, good. All settled then?"

"Emma can wear pink," Mimi announced.

There went the smiles. The girls deflated like balloons, and as the air left them, a strange rustling sound was heard from the fabric moving.

"Pea green and pink?" Margo wrinkled her nose.

Yes, pea green. Leave it to Margo to find such an accurate description of this color.

"Why not?" Mimi asked. "You'll look like flowers. The petals and the stems."

"Petals and stems," Melanie murmured across the room. She met Abby's eyes and mouthed "Sorry!" before disappearing again.

Margo closed her eyes, and Abby could tell she was either on the brink of tears or a headache.

"If you insist on green," she finally said, as she shuffled through the rack, "then what about this nice...sea foam?" she added weakly.

Yes, this was dire. So dire that Margo was actually going with the worst cliché there was when it came to bridesmaid dresses.

"Now why on earth would I pick sea foam of all colors?" Mimi remarked, clearly losing her patience.

Well, let's see, Abby thought. They lived in Oyster Bay, which was a seaside community. "Isn't this a beach wedding?"

"No, it is not," Mimi surprised them all by saying.

Abby couldn't tell who was more shocked by this revelation. Herself or Bridget.

"But I thought you were getting married in the backyard of the house," Bridget said, blinking rapidly. Abby couldn't tell if it was from anger or relief. After all, when Margo had gotten married at the inn last month, Bridget had felt the stress even more than the bride.

"No, I said an outdoor wedding. You filled in the rest," Mimi said airily. "Earl and I want something more personal. We're getting married at Serenity Hills. In the beautiful garden courtyard, surrounded by flowers."

"Hence the reason for these dresses?" Abby asked miserably.

Mimi wagged her finger at her. "You always were a smart cookie. These two never give you enough credit!"

Abby wasn't sure if this was a compliment or an insult. Given the way the day was going, she decided to look at the bright side, even if it was a reach.

"But, I thought…I thought…Mimi, we all met for dinner and discussed this." Now Bridget really did look overwhelmed. Her cheeks were all pink and her hair seemed suddenly a mess, and it didn't take a genius to know what she wanted to say and didn't. "I already rented a tent!"

"Well, the tent can go in the courtyard," Mimi said, as if that were that.

The sisters stood, completely bewildered. All this time

they'd been led to believe that Mimi hated living at Serenity Hills. They'd all felt guilty over it.

"We're getting married at Serenity Hills. Pudgie will be the ring bearer. Emma will be the flower girl, and you will be my bridesmaids. Bridget, as you are the oldest, you will be my maid of honor."

Bridget stared at Mimi for a long moment. "Thank you?" The response came out like a question, not a statement.

The girls glanced at one another, not sure what to say next. Finally, it was Margo who spoke. "And the flowers? We were going to discuss those next time I visited."

"Whatever goes well with these dresses," Mimi remarked.

So there it was. There was no getting out of it. They would wear the avocado dresses, complete with a ball gown skirt and a giant bow at the back and ruffles along the neckline.

Abby turned and frowned at herself in the mirror, trying to will herself to find something likeable in the dress and failing miserably. Melanie was offering condolences as she ushered Margo and Bridget into the dressing rooms, no doubt afraid to lose the business of all their friends after this. Abby was just about to join her sisters in the dressing room to have a much-needed vent when she saw him. There, in the mirror, was the reflection of Zach, looking up at her.

She turned to the window before she had time to think of what she was doing, and sure enough, there he was, watching her as if he had been doing so for a while. His hands were stuffed in his pockets and there was a grin on his face she never had been able to resist.

"Nice dress!" he mouthed, and maybe because she'd lost the fight, or maybe because she couldn't fight anymore, or maybe because a small part of her held out hope that this time it could all be different, she smiled back.

*

Zach was sitting outside on the bench when she emerged with her sisters and Mimi a few minutes later. Mimi was discussing flower options with Margo, and Bridget was saying something about needing to pick up Emma from Ryan's. All three women were far too distracted to notice that after Abby waved good-bye, she didn't head in the direction of home.

She hovered in front of the bench, at a nice, safe, five-foot distance, because it would be rude to keep walking. And running had gotten her nowhere.

"Nice dress," Zach said again. There was a gleam in his eye that bordered on devilish, and despite herself, Abby grinned.

"Try telling my sisters that," she said. "But then, they don't need to worry about not being asked to dance at the reception."

"I'd ask you to dance," Zach said, and damn it if her heart didn't patter a bit over that thought. There'd never been weddings or even formal parties back when they were dating, but there had been music, and sometimes that was all it took for Zach to reach out, put a hand on her waist, and pull her close, in one effortless movement. If she closed her eyes she could still feel the beat of his pulse against her chest, the warm strength of his body close to her. The feeling that she'd hoped would last forever.

"Well, it's a small affair. Second wedding and all."

"And you are the blushing bridesmaid." His grin was positively wicked now.

"Go on and laugh all you want," Abby said. "I'm just honored to be a part of the big day."

"You can't lie to me, Abby," Zach teased, but there was something in his eyes that said he was dead serious, too. "I know you too well."

That he did. And she didn't know how to feel about that. In all these years, no one else had ever come close to understanding her the way Zach could. Maybe it had been when they met, a unique time in her life when so much changed, or maybe it was because he'd cared to peel back the layers and see who was underneath, or maybe it was sheer time…day after day of being together. He wasn't just her boyfriend. He was her closest friend. As close as her sisters. Closer even.

"Fine. You win. I hate the dress." Who wouldn't? "Your sister hates it, too, I'll have you know. She couldn't stop apologizing."

"But you'll still wear it?"

"It's Mimi's wedding." Abby shrugged. She gave him a long look. "It's what you do for people you care about."

After bribery, guilt-trips, and all other means of manipulation were gone, of course.

She shifted the weight on her feet. He was staring at her, and it was making her uncomfortable. She didn't like looking at that face. Those eyes. Those hands. They still pulled her in, and made her long for something. "So…waiting for Melanie?"

"Waiting for you, actually."

Oh.

"I saw you in the window and, well, I never could resist a girl in green." He looked at her, and for a moment, her breath caught.

She'd been wearing a green scarf the day they'd met. Well, not the day they'd met—after all, they'd both grown up here in Oyster Bay. But the day that they'd connected, the day he'd noticed her, walked with her, talked with her long after they'd reached the library, and then later invited her for a coffee at the shop around the corner…She'd been wearing her green scarf. And he remembered.

"Free this afternoon?" Zach asked suddenly, and Abby felt herself stiffen. She tried to think of an excuse, a plausible one, but she was a terrible liar, and besides, Zach was right, he knew her too well. He didn't even wait for a response to say, "Spend the day with me."

"Zach…"

"Nothing formal," he promised, holding up a hand.

"Just…you and me. Like old times."

Like old times. She hated how much the thought appealed to her. Nearly as much as the hope that shone in his eyes.

She dragged a toe against the pavement, trying to summon a plausible excuse and failing miserably. "What did you have in mind?"

He grinned and stood before she had time to back away. He was close, so close that she could smell that soap again, and it clung to her, in her memory, bringing a rush of emotions all at once, of happier, carefree days. The kind he wanted to have again. Today.

"You hungry?" he asked.

She hesitated, even though she'd missed lunch and the afternoon was slipping by. "I thought you said this was casual."

"Walk with me," he said, reaching out to skim her hand. She kept her hand low at her side, but he didn't pull back. Instead, his thumb grazed hers, sending a shiver down her spine. She met his eye, trying to will him to back away and give her space. To let her be. But his gaze was steady, and when he took her hand, lacing her fingers in his, it felt like old times. It felt better than old times. It felt…right.

"Where are we going?" she asked warily.

"You'll like it. I promise." Sensing her reserve, he grinned a little wider. "Trust me," he said, and for some reason, she did.

*

The Clam Shack was an old institution, open only from May through September, in an old shack down on Fisherman's Beach. It switched hands every decade or so, but the recipes stayed the same.

"I've missed the lobster rolls you can get around here," Zach said as he sat on the sand, Abby a safe three feet beside him, he noticed.

"You never came back to visit in all those years," Abby observed, striking at the guilt chord that was always present these days.

"Work," he said ruefully.

"It always was important to you," she seemed to accuse. She paused to take a bite of her sandwich. "So why'd you leave?"

"I couldn't take it, I guess." He shrugged, and, taking one last bite of his roll, balled up the wax paper in his hands. "It was exciting at first, travelling around, covering the action, feeling like you were a part of something."

"But it's what you always wanted to do," she pointed out.

This is where she was wrong. Where everyone was wrong. "It's what I always thought I wanted to do," he corrected.

"No," Abby said, shaking her head. "It was all you talked about in college. It was your passion. It was your goal. You worked so hard. You were willing to give up everything, even—" She stopped herself, and looked down at the basket of fries that was in her lap.

"Even you?" he said, feeling his jaw pulse as he gritted his teeth. "I was wrong, Abby. About so many things."

He stared at her, waiting for her to meet his eye, but she wouldn't.

"What changed for you? What made you want to quit?"

Quit. That word. But he supposed that's exactly what he'd done. He'd given up. First on Oyster Bay. Then on Abby. Then on his career. Then on himself.

"It was a buildup, really. I went where the stories were, where the tough stories were, and…I couldn't compartmentalize." Instead he'd walked away, feeling helpless, and staring at the glow of his computer screen long after he'd sent off his story, his mind still fresh with what he'd seen and learned. With things he couldn't change. Violence. Destruction. Hopelessness.

"Because you cared," she said, giving him a little smile.

He appreciated it, more than she could know. It was a sign of forgiveness, a sign that perhaps he should forgive himself. "Didn't have what it took," he replied curtly. "I wanted to make a difference. And I didn't."

"Now that's not fair," Abby said, bridging the gap between them to elbow him softly. "Every interview you did, every article you wrote, someone read that."

"And then tossed it in the trash." He shook his head.

"How do you know? For all you know one of your articles touched someone enough for them to take action. Enough for them to…prompt change."

He wanted to believe it, so badly.

"What does your family say about it?"

"My family?" Zach almost laughed. "My mom is just happy I'm back in town, and my dad just asks what's going on at the paper. I think my mom instructed him not to ask any questions—she'd rather just accept the fact that I'm here." No doubt a part of her knew that something had brought him back, and that it might eventually lead him away again. It was easier to ignore what you didn't want to see.

He closed his eyes. But sometimes, it was right there, in your face, and there was no hiding from it.

"I can't do it anymore. The things I saw. The violence. The destruction. The world is a rough place. Not like here."

"Oh, I know it's a rough place," Abby said, raising her eyebrows at him. "Only my experience was right here, in Oyster Bay. This is where my family was torn apart, where my sisters and I lost our parents, where Mimi lost her son. Where Bridget lost a husband and had a baby to raise mostly on her own."

He'd never really thought of it that way, and now he felt shame. "When you wanted to come back here, I didn't want to stop you. You stuck by people. You put them first. And seeing what you have with your family…I guess you could say it makes me think about everything I gave up."

"And what I gave up?" She stared at him in disbelief.

"I gave up you, Zach. I gave up the opportunity to travel and see the world and...experience life!" She shook her head. "Back in college, you always knew what you wanted to do. You were so sure of your path. So certain of your future. I wasn't like that."

"You followed your heart, Abby," he said, feeling his chest pull when he looked at her sad smile. "I always admired that about you."

"And you?"

He shrugged. Heaved a sigh. "I set out to make a difference. To have a voice."

"Well, maybe there's another way," Abby said. "What does Melanie say?"

"Melanie's caught up in her own troubles at the moment," Zach said. "I didn't want to burden her with mine."

"What about using your skills for something else? Taking that passion and moving it in a different direction?"

"You mean you don't think I'm going to open people's eyes on world events by working at the *Oyster Bay Gazette*?" He frowned at her. "I'm sorry again, Abby. About the article. It was my first week and I was asked to cover the assignment and...I'm not used to being nice."

"You're used to being honest," she said with a sigh. She set her food to the side and folded her arms over her knees as she looked out onto the waves that hit the sand and then rolled away. "A batch of my scones overcooked that day. It's no one's fault but my own. Truth is that it just tapped into my worst fears, I guess you could say."

"But you're fearless."

"Me?" she laughed. "No. I'm cautious. To a fault. I didn't even tell my own sisters how much I loved baking and cooking until I was runner-up in the fall pie baking contest. And even then I only spoke up because Bridget had a catering crisis at the inn and needed all hands on deck. And when everyone seemed to like what I made...Well, it felt good. So I took a risk."

"See? You followed your heart. And it paid off," Zach said.

"Not necessarily," Abby said. "Bridget took some convincing, and even now, it's still a trial period of sorts. I still haven't told her about the food truck at the festival."

Zach knew an opportunity when he saw one. "Hey, let me help out at the food truck. As a way of making things up to you."

She looked at him quizzically. "You'd do that for me?"

"Of course I would. I'd...I'd do anything for you, Abby." He swallowed hard, knowing it was the truth even if it hadn't been seven years ago. Back then he was hungry, eager, he needed to do what he'd set out to do. But now he'd done that, and he'd seen. It left him empty and unsatisfied, and...unhappy. And Abby, well, she always made him happy.

They were staring at each other, as if each waiting for the other to say something, or make a move, to take the action that would move them in one direction or another.

He held his breath, waiting for the right moment, but it was too late.

"Well, I should probably go get a start on my recipes then." Abby was scrambling to her feet faster than he could react, but he couldn't let her slip away, not this time.

"So you're going to let me help?" he asked when they were standing face to face.

She brushed away a strand of hair that was blowing in the breeze. In the clear afternoon light, her eyes were a vibrant green, and the dusting of freckles on her nose was prominent. "Are you just doing this to clear your conscience, Zach?" She turned her nose up, her mouth pert as she waited for his reply.

He could banter with her, drag out this…dance. Or he could be honest. The way he'd been trained to be. The way he wanted to be.

"Come on, Abby, no more games," he said softly. "I'm here. I'm back. I made a mistake. Then. Now. And I'm trying everything I can to make it all up to you. If you'll let me."

She chewed on her bottom lip, looking up at him warily, and then finally nodded.

He stepped forward, set a hand on her waist, the rush of that contact making his heart speed up. He waited for her to back up, to turn and run, but this time she didn't. He leaned down, until their mouths touched, and then he kissed her, slowly, just like he had kissed her a thousand times before, only it had never been as wonderful as this time.

He wrapped his arms tighter around her waist, pulling her against his chest until he didn't know where his body ended and hers began, taking in her heat, her warmth, the sweet strawberry scent of that shampoo she still used.

"You didn't run," he said, when they broke apart.

She gave him a mischievous smile and looked down almost shyly. "And neither did you."

He laughed under his breath as they walked back toward the steps that would lead them into town. He hadn't run. But could he stay put, here in Oyster Bay? It was something he'd have to figure out. And soon.

Chapter Eleven

Bridget was in a tense mood the next morning, something to do with Ryan cancelling on an afternoon fishing trip he'd been promising to Emma for three weeks. It wasn't unusual for him to say that something had come up at the restaurant, but each time it did, Emma broke down into tears and Bridget fell eerily silent.

Abby supposed she could hold off, talk to Bridget tomorrow instead, when her mood was better, and all that. Really, timing was important here. But something told Abby that if she kept this inside much longer she might lose all nerve. She'd prepared her speech, rehearsed it first in the shower and then the entire bike ride across town, working out her nerves on the pedals, extra careful not to slip this time.

She balled a fist at her side as Bridget walked into the

kitchen with a carafe and filled it from the fresh pot of coffee. Breakfast was technically over, everyone had been served, without complaints, and now all that was left to do was to keep the coffee flowing while she cleaned up the kitchen and prepped a bit for tomorrow.

She usually did this quickly, chopping vegetables and cross-referencing the pantry with her ingredient lists, eager to get home and on with her day, but today she dragged it out, lingering, working up her nerve as much as she was trying to convince herself to hold off…

"Bridget?" She startled herself so much that her entire body seemed to stiffen. She stared at her sister, who casually looked at her, eyebrows raised in question, a pleasant-enough expression on her face.

She tried to think of an excuse, a question she could ask, something to back out of the moment, but she couldn't do it. She had to talk to Bridget. Now. Or she'd be sick the rest of the day worrying about tomorrow.

In her mind, it hadn't gone like this. In her mind, she and Bridget sat at the big island, sipping coffee and talking about long-term plans. She was supposed to start off with asking about upcoming reservations and then scheduling her formal trial period review, a good way to ease into the scary stuff.

Instead, she blurted, "I meant to tell you that I volunteered Harper House Inn for a food truck at Summer Fest."

Bridget seemed momentarily confused. "A food truck?

But we're an inn…"

"That serves food," Abby pointed out the obvious.

"A bed and breakfast," Bridget said, blinking rapidly. She was processing this, and that wasn't necessarily a good thing.

"It's a good way to get our name out there. I thought." Now Abby wasn't so sure what she thought. Now she wondered if the reason she hadn't told Bridget right away was because she feared this reaction.

"You should have run this by me first," Bridget said, setting the carafe down.

Abby swallowed hard. Her cheeks were heating and her heart was beating so hard she half wondered if Bridget could hear it across the room. "I was at the planning meeting and I got put on the spot. I didn't realize you would object."

"It's not that I object, but I would have liked to have been told. This is my business, Abby. I need to know everything that is going on with it."

Of course. It was Bridget's inn. And even though Abby had grown up under this roof, and made Christmas cookies in this very kitchen, the business—and the house—were Bridget's.

And now she'd gone and made things worse.

"I can tell them I won't do it," she tried.

"The festival is next weekend," Bridget replied, sighing. "What are you planning on doing? Do I have any say?"

"Of course you have say!" But the truth was that Abby

hadn't considered that. She'd just assumed that Bridget would go along with what she'd planned. "I was going to offer three dishes to keep it simple. Something portable and easy to make in large batches. Mini quiches, breakfast bruschetta, and, um…" Did she dare say it? "Blueberry scones."

She waited for Bridget to argue with that, but, after a small pause of consideration, Bridget shrugged again. "Sounds like you've thought it through."

Crisis averted! Abby smiled in relief. "And it won't interfere with my hours here. The festival doesn't start until noon and I can do a lot of prep work the day before."

"Did you need to use the kitchen?" Bridget asked, saving Abby the worry of having to ask.

"That would be great, thanks." She jumped. She almost forgot the best part. "And all proceeds go to the inn, of course. I wasn't doing this for myself, Bridge…this was for us. For the business."

"It's a good idea," Bridget said, reaching for the carafe again. "But next time, check with me first, okay?"

"Of course." Abby nodded solemnly until Bridget had left the room, and then she fist-pumped triumphantly. Okay, so she hadn't gotten up the nerve to ask about her trial period ending, but she'd deal with that next week, and after the festival. After all, come this time next Sunday, she may have just turned around the inn's reputation and earned some newfound respect from her sister.

Things were on the up and up.

*

Zach looked over at his mother, who was doing her best to encourage Melanie to hang the fat striped ribbon from the lampposts a little higher. Melanie's ponytail was coming undone and her cheeks were a dark pink from the combination of the exertion and the afternoon heat. From the look on her face, she wished she was on her recliner, a bowl of pretzels in her lap, rather than helping out with the festival setup.

"Come on, Melanie, a little higher! Or maybe I could ask Brad Norris to come help?"she asked hopefully.

Melanie shot Zach a look of such fury that he had to laugh out loud. Melanie wouldn't be interested in Brad, and besides, he and Sarah seemed to be really hitting it off since the night at Dunley's.

"I figured out why you roped me into this volunteer stuff," Melanie accused, when she finally got off the ladder.

He looked at her in amusement. "And what is that?"

"You wanted to have a reason to hang around Abby Harper," she said, catching him by such surprise, he was momentarily speechless.

"I saw you talking to her outside my shop," she continued, a knowing smile forming on her mouth.

"I can promise you that I did not know Abby was helping out with the festival when Mom suggested we participate, because I must remind you, it was Mom who insisted, not me."

Melanie crossed her arms, not looking convinced in the least. "Well, seems to me that I got the wrong end of the stick on this one. You get to hang around Abby, and I get…Brad Norris?" She laughed, and Zach joined in, out of relief more than anything else. The last thing he needed was for his broken-hearted sister to go falling for someone who wasn't even available.

"Mom won't stop trying to set me up. And encouraging me to do things. You know I've never been much of a joiner. That's her thing."

"She just does it because she cares," Zach said. But he understood. Melanie needed a little space. He would honor that. "I'm sorry for dragging you into this. I was worried about you and I thought it would give you a reason to get out of the house. But it's okay to take some time for yourself, too."

She looked surprise. "Thank you." She eyed him for a moment. "Is that what you're doing back here? Taking some time for yourself? Or are you back to stay?"

"Melanie!" It was their mother calling, waving a fistful of ribbon in the air.

Melanie turned back to Zach and rolled her eyes. "You do owe me for this."

With a wave at his exasperated sister, Zach went off in search of Brad, who was setting up chairs and tables in the town green, near where the food trucks would be stationed.

"Seems like a lot of setup for an event that's still a week away," Brad said, a little breathlessly.

"It's the only time people have to help," Zach said, recalling his mother's words. "Besides, it drags out the fun."

Brad set down a stack of chairs and cocked an eyebrow. "Fun?"

Zach jutted his chin to Sarah, who was setting up the kid's corner, noticing with a jolt that Abby was now beside her. She spotted him and waved across the grass, and he did the same, the memory of their kiss last night rushing back to him.

He lifted a chair from the stack and began unfolding it, forcing his attention back to Brad. "Come on, now. Looks like you're having fun being here with Sarah."

"Yeah, about that."

Uh-oh. Zach watched as Brad set down the chairs, not bothering to unfold any. "You know how I was thinking of switching over to coaching? Maybe heading up the high school team next fall?"

Brad had mentioned this around the office a few times, and when they went for drinks, too. "Yes."

"Well, I got a coaching position. In Portland," he finished.

In other words, he was leaving Oyster Bay. Of course, he was moving forward, pursuing his dreams, whereas Zach…Zach had given up on his.

"So you and Sarah…"

"It can't go anywhere. She's a great girl and all, but, you understand."

Zach did. All too well. "Sometimes you've got to take an opportunity when it knocks."

"And it sounds like a great opportunity," Brad said.

"Absolutely. Besides, what opportunities are there in this town?" None, not unless you were fine running one of the shops or working down at the docks. Even the nearest hospital was thirty minutes away in Shelter Port; the town only had one doctor, who was never allowed to get sick. Still, Abby had gotten him thinking last night, about less traditional methods, about other ways he might be able to do what he'd set out to do, all those years ago.

He bent down, reaching for another stack of chairs, when he saw her. He started to smile, until he saw the expression on her face. Her eyes were wide and her mouth was pinched, and before he could even say hello, Sarah called out to her, and she turned and walked away.

Chapter Twelve

The next morning, Abby arrived at the inn with a heart heavier than she'd had the day after the review was posted. She'd given in. Dared to believe again. And where had it gotten her?

Now Zach was leaving Oyster Bay, off to seek "opportunities," and she was…well, she was here, in her hometown, where she wanted to be. She should have known it would never be good enough for Zach. That she'd never be good enough.

With a sigh, she set her bag of ingredients on the counter. Usually she looked forward to weekday mornings when she could try out new recipes with the lighter load of guests, but today even the thrill of trying a twist on eggs Benedict couldn't lift her mood.

"Everything okay, Auntie Abby?" Emma came into

the kitchen, her little face pinched with worry.

Abby tousled her niece's hair, noticing as she always did how silky it was. Often Bridget braided it, or brushed it into a ponytail, but today Emma's hair was still loose at her shoulders and a little tangled from sleep.

"Oh, just a bit down in the dumps today." Abby's voice caught, and she blinked rapidly, willing herself not to cry. That was just what she needed to cement her exit from the kitchen of the Harper House Inn. Nope, not going for another strike when she was already dangerously close to number three.

She opened the fridge and pulled out a carton of orange juice. She poured a glass for Emma and one for herself. Sugar might help clear her head, or at least give her a little boost for the morning, after which, she would be going home to her apartment to crawl back into bed for the rest of the day. Oh, yes.

"Did you lose something?" Emma asked, sipping her juice.

Abby knew that Emma was implying something tangible and replaceable, like a stuffed animal or a charm bracelet or a sparkly pencil with a funny eraser. She nodded slowly anyway. "I did lose something."

"You want me to help you find it?" Emma offered, always so happy to help.

"No, honey," Abby said sadly. "This is something that is gone forever." Something that had really been gone a long time ago, so why did she ever go searching for it again?

Emma's blue eyes sprang open. "Gone forever?" She went completely silent, as if she hadn't considered this possibility before. "But…you can't find it again?"

"I did find it again. Believe it or not this is the second time I've lost this."

"The second time?" Emma's mouth gaped'. "Well, then, that wasn't very responsible."

Despite her mood, Abby laughed out loud. Emma was a quick study, and she spent a lot of time with her mother, enough so that some of Bridget's lectures rubbed off on her. Still, coming from Emma the delivery wasn't quite so tough to hear. Even if it was the cold hard truth.

"It wasn't responsible," she agreed. Not in the least. She'd known what Zach was capable of, what he prioritized and cared about most, and she'd still walked right into his arms.

"I'll make you a card to cheer you up," Emma offered. She set her empty juice glass on the counter and ran off in search of her paper and markers, which would no doubt keep her busy until Bridget took her to camp.

Abby started cracking eggs and slicing English muffins. This sort of work was typically therapeutic, a sure way to relax and lose herself for a few minutes, but today she was distracted—she broke a yoke and lost a few shells in the eggs too.

She cursed under her breath, just as Bridget was entering the kitchen, as luck would have it.

"Everything okay?"

"Peachy," Abby said, grinning, but she knew from the look on her sister's face that she wasn't buying it.

"Emma said she's making you a card. She said you lost something you can never find again." She raised an eyebrow. An invitation to talk.

"Zach is leaving town," Abby replied. There. She'd said it. Opened up. Why not? There was nothing to speculate now, nothing to hope for, nothing that either of her sisters could tease her about. They'd seen her heartache before. They'd assume this was the same.

Besides, she couldn't think of an excuse quick enough. So the truth would have to do.

Bridget frowned and dropped onto a barstool. "You really had something with him, didn't you?"

Abby fished the shells from the bowl of eggs, refusing to meet her sister's eye. "It was a long time ago."

"First love," Bridget said, giving her a knowing smile. "And all these other guys never came close, did they?"

"I tried," Abby confessed. "I tried to convince myself." Tried to hide. To deny what she really wanted. What she deserved.

It was easier that way. Less scary than putting yourself out there. Risking it all.

"Zach's a good guy," Bridget said. "I can see why he'd be hard to get over."

"Well," Abby said, refusing to give in to that kind of sentiment. "It doesn't matter. He put his work first back then and he put his work first again." She eyed her sister, hating to even bring up such a delicate topic. "You know, he wrote that review."

Bridget stared at her in disbelief. "Because he was mad at you?"

"No, not because he was mad at me," Abby huffed, but then she considered that maybe he had been a bit mad at her. And she had chosen to be shy about her position, defensive really. And why? Because she was afraid he wouldn't support her? Wouldn't understand? Or because she was afraid she wasn't good enough? "He didn't know I was the cook here." She should have told him. She should have been proud.

"Why didn't you tell him?" Bridget looked confused, and all that Abby could do was shrug in response. After a pause, Bridget said quietly, "You know what your problem is, don't you?"

Now she had Abby's full attention. She stared at her sister, heart thumping as she waited for her to elaborate, her mouth too dry to say anything else.

"You lack confidence, Abby." Bridget shook her head. "It's amazing, because you are so talented. So smart and funny and outgoing. But you need to learn to believe in yourself."

"Then why were you so hesitant to let me work here?" Abby asked.

"Because you don't stick with things," Bridget replied, and as much as it hurt to hear, Abby knew it was the truth. "When things get real, you run. Honestly, I was a little surprised you didn't quit on me after that bad review."

"Quit on you?" Abby could barely believe what she was hearing.

"Isn't it a valid concern?" Bridget asked. "When things get complicated, you don't stick around. It's been about fun to you for a long time now."

True, it had been about fun to her. Enjoying the moment. Living for today. Not worrying about the future or thinking about the past. With jobs. With relationships.

"You had me really worried," Bridget admitted. "I've come to depend on having you here. I like having you here. The guests do too."

"And me!" Emma cried, skipping into the kitchen, holding a card that had a big sun and flowers drawn on it.

Bridget laughed and gave her daughter a squeeze. "Grab your backpack for camp, honey. I'll be ready in five minutes."

Abby watched Emma dash off again, still trying to process what her sister had told her. "So...the trial period?"

"It was just as much for you as it was for me," Bridget said. "I always wanted this to work. I think we make a pretty good team. That is, if you agree."

Abby tried to make sense of what her sister was saying. "You mean, the trial period is over?"

Bridget nodded. "The trial period is over. That is...if you really want to stay?"

"Really want to stay?" But then Abby understood. She

flitted from job to job. From guy to guy. But that wasn't her. It never had been. "I'm done running, Bridget. I'm done trying to stop myself from caring and investing." She'd taken a risk. Gotten her feelings hurt. But she was still here.

"Honestly, I had to ensure you'd stick around for at least that long, but I can see that you've changed, Abby. You're a fighter."

A fighter. Was that what she was? Somehow a part of her still felt like a quitter.

"Well," Bridget sighed and pushed back from the counter. "I'm off to take Emma to camp. When I get back maybe we can discuss Mimi's wedding a little more before we go visit her this afternoon?"

"That would be great," Abby said, cracking an egg with newfound enthusiasm. She was still smiling, long after the door had closed and Bridget's car could be heard crunching on the gravel driveway.

She looked around the kitchen, her heavy heart lifting inch by inch.

She was home, in every way possible. And this time, she wasn't quitting. Not on this kitchen. Not on herself.

And maybe, not even on her heart.

*

Melanie eyed the open suitcase when she emerged from her bedroom, her work clothes replaced by her usual pajama pants, tee shirt, and fading peach-colored terry cloth robe which was starting to show signs of wear.

Zach eyed the hole on the sleeve and wondered if he should point it out, but decided against it. Melanie was defensive of her current state, and he wasn't going to question it. If it lasted another two months, then measures would be taken. Besides, he'd seen some of her old spirit returning. After all, it wasn't like their mother had dragged her out of her apartment and over to the festival setup yesterday. She'd gone, and deep down, she'd probably enjoyed it. Even if she hadn't admitted so.

The festival setup. He hadn't liked the way that had ended, with Abby leaving before they'd even had a chance to talk.

"I'm just going to New York for a few days," he told his sister.

"I knew it wouldn't last long," she said, strutting past him into the kitchen, where she poured herself a glass of wine from the tap that was attached to the box she kept on the left-hand side of the fridge. It was a zinfandel today. Too sweet for his liking.

"I mean it, Mel," Zach stopped packing and stared at his sister until she looked at him properly. "I'm coming back on Friday. There are just some things I need to wrap up."

Melanie dropped onto her recliner and studied him for a moment. "You mean to tell me you think you could be happy, here in Oyster Bay?"

He'd thought about it a lot over the past few days, and he nodded with confidence. "I do."

"But why now? Before you couldn't wait to get out, see the world, make—"

He held up his hand. "Make a difference. I know, I know." Zach dropped onto the sofa. "Truth is, maybe you don't have to go so far to do that. Maybe this time I can make a difference right here. Have an impact, just in a smaller way." He shrugged. "And maybe it will mean even more."

After all, wasn't that what Abby had done? Put her family first, made a difference in their lives, rather than trying to reach every person in the world? He'd thought about her words. He'd thought about her choices. And he finally had a plan. And this was one that he knew he'd be sticking to.

"So you're moving back here." Melanie still didn't seem convinced.

"I'll be moving into an apartment at the start of the month," he told her. "Brad Norris is moving out, and I'm moving in." If that wasn't serendipity, he didn't know what was.

"Brad!" Melanie rolled her eyes to the ceiling and slumped dramatically against the back of her chair. "At least with him moving away, Mom can get off my back about him. He's so not my type."

"Anyone else you have your eye on?" Zach asked, as he resumed packing.

"Like I'd tell you," she said. "But no." Her voice seemed a little sad and silence fell over the room.

"So you're really coming back?" she finally asked again,

as he zippered his suitcase closed and set it on the floor near the front door.

"I am. If you'll have me."

Melanie grinned. "We're family, Zach. That door is always open to you."

He didn't dare admit to her that he'd been counting on it. But it still felt damn good to hear.

*

Margo was already in Mimi's room when Bridget and Abby arrived at Serenity Hills that evening after dropping Emma off with Ryan for a few hours, and from the ruddy complexion to her face, Abby could only assume that Pudgie was on the prowl again.

"I know it's just a cat," Margo whispered almost tearfully, "but I swear that thing has it out for me." She held out her hand, which sure enough had a fresh scratch. "Mimi let him climb the drapes again. Please tell me you won't let him be in the wedding. I can just see him climbing a tree branch and taking a leap at my head."

Margo grabbed Bridget by both elbows, her expression almost pained, and Abby was reminded of the natural order of their family. Even though they were all grown up, and even though Margo was married and running a successful business of her own, Bridget would always be the one she turned to. And Bridget always pulled through.

"Mimi," Bridget crossed the small room to sit next to the old rocking chair that once sat on the back porch of what was now the inn. For as long as Abby could remember, Mimi would sit on that chair, facing the sea, often with a blanket on her lap and a book in her hands. Sometimes an hour would lapse before she turned a page, because the view was just as interesting as the story, she said. "Let's go over the details of the wedding guest list."

"I know who I want and I know who I don't," Mimi said firmly. "Pudgie is invited and that Esther Preston is not."

Now Abby had heard enough. "Mimi," she said, coming to sit next to Bridget, "I think you should know that Esther's granddaughter and I have become friends. She's a very nice girl who would probably love to come to the wedding and meet some new people in town. And maybe you could...extend an olive branch."

"And invite Esther to my wedding? I'd sooner dress Pudgie like a girl, thank you very much!"

Abby blinked, not exactly sure how to respond to any of that, and, following the suit of Margo, looked beseechingly at Bridget.

Bridget sighed, but turned back to Mimi. "And what is it that you have against Esther exactly? Other than the pudding cup and the flower fiasco."

"You heard about that, too?" Abby muttered.

Bridget turned and nodded her head. "Who do you think got the call from the management office?"

Abby heard Margo snort in laughter and had to bite her own lip to keep from laughing.

"Esther must be what? Ninety?" Bridget looked at

Mimi frankly. Her patience was wearing thin.

"She's eighty-eight and she has the hots for my man," Mimi said, pinching her lips tight. "First it was Mitch. Then it was that male nurse that you had your eye on, Abby. And now it is Earl."

Abby blinked in confusion. That male nurse—she never had caught his name—couldn't have been a day over thirty-five. She opened her mouth and then shut it again. Who was she to argue?

"Yes, but Earl loves you," Bridget reminded her gently. "And maybe what Esther really needs is a friend."

Mimi seemed to mull this over, but by the guilty expression that took over, it was clear that Bridget was getting through to her.

"We can even come with you when you invite her to the wedding," Margo added, looking wistfully at the door. Any excuse to get away from Pudgie.

"Fine then," Mimi said with great reluctance. "You lot always had a way of wearing me down."

"And you love us for it," Bridget said with a smile that shone with relief.

The sisters all eyed each other as they helped move Mimi to her wheelchair, Pudgie content to stay secure in her lap, under the wary gaze of Margo. Abby led the way, even though Esther's room was only next door. The door was closed, and for a moment Abby wasn't sure if they should come back another time. Esther might be asleep or—

Bridget took the liberty of knocking. "Mrs. Preston? It's Bridget Harper. Margaret Harper's granddaughter? I was hoping we could chat for a moment."

"If this is about that flower business, she should know I'm keeping an eye on her! I know a thief when I see one!"

Margo and Abby exchanged wide-eyed stares while Bridget flashed a rueful look at Mimi. "It's not about the flowers or...anything else. I just came by to say hello. I promise."

There was shuffling on the other side of the door and, after what felt like an eternity, the door creaked open.

Esther stood there, her blue eyes sharp as an eagle's as she peered at them. "Yes?"

"Our grandmother has something she would like to say to you," Margo said. When Mimi didn't speak, she gave her a little nudge on the shoulder.

After a dramatic huff, Mimi said, "My granddaughters think it's high time we make amends. Abby here is friends with your granddaughter Sarah—"

"Abby!" Esther's eyes lit up. "Sarah speaks nonstop of you. Of course I had no idea that you were related to *Margaret*." Her lips pinched on that for a moment.

Abby shifted nervously on her feet. "Well, Sarah and I didn't want to cause any more tension," she promised. "But seeing as we're such friends, we thought it would be nice if you two could be as well." She looked around the hall, spotting the activities sign down near the elevators. "After all, wouldn't it be nice to have someone to go to

Bingo with sometime?"

"Well, you have Earl for that," Esther said, a little sadly.

"Bingo stresses Earl out. Too much luck in the game and not enough strategy," Mimi said. She paused, then finally tossed up her hands. "What can I say? These girls have worn me down."

Esther grinned. "I know the feeling. Sarah was in here all last night crying her eyes out. I thought this was supposed to be a rest home!"

Despite the bonding moment, Abby grew concerned. "What's wrong with Sarah?"

"Oh, troubles of the heart, I'm afraid. That poor girl never did have luck with men." Esther clucked her tongue.

"Tell me about it," Mimi offered. She jutted her thumb at Bridget and Margo. "These two are both divorced and the youngest one may never settle down. It's her red hair, I tell you. Fiery spirit."

And the good will was officially up. Abby looked at her sisters, who were backing away, eyes rolling now, deciding it was time to leave. Their deed for the day was up, the world was set right again. Well, aside for Abby. And Sarah.

As they walked back out into the summer sun, Abby considered that somewhere across town, someone's heart might be breaking just as much as her own. But that maybe, somehow, there was still hope for both of them.

Chapter Thirteen

On the morning of the Summer Fest, Abby woke at four o'clock sharp, and she didn't even snooze her alarm. She pedaled to the inn, where she brewed the coffee before Bridget even shuffled into the kitchen, whipped up some blueberry pancakes and a breakfast hash, and simultaneously finished making her offerings for the food truck. The mini scones and quiches baked quickly, especially since she'd prepped the night before, and Margo could be counted on for watching the timer, setting everything to cool, and then packing each item in the large plastic containers they would use to transport the food. The breakfast bruschetta would be made on site—something that Abby only worried about when she allowed herself to, but right now, she didn't have the time to do that. Right now she'd have to rely on her old self, the one who was more carefree and less cautious. She'd decided (optimistically) on twelve dozen of everything, and whatever didn't get sold could be donated to Serenity Hills.

She'd worked all week, grateful to be so busy that it kept her mind from wandering, and by the time breakfast service was over, she was ready. Not a burnt scone in the batch, she thought, with a slightly sad smile.

"There won't be room for me in the car," Margo said as she helped Abby and Bridget carry everything out of the kitchen. "Why don't I stay here with Emma?"

"I'll be back in a bit," Bridget promised, and gave Abby a grin. "Ready?"

"Ready as I'll ever be," Abby said, even though her stomach was starting to feel funny.

"You show this town who makes the best blueberry scones," Margo said through the open window.

"I intend to," Abby said, only somehow it didn't matter quite so much anymore. Zach had written the review. He had turned her life upside down. And now he was gone. He couldn't rectify the havoc he'd done even if he tried. And he hadn't tried, had he?

She checked her phone a hundred times all week, jumped every time the doorbell to her apartment rang, and felt her heart speed up every time she walked down Main Street. But there was no word from Zach.

Life had gone back to the way it was before he'd come back. Only somehow, it was different.

"Everything okay?" Bridget asked as they pulled to a

stop near the town green—a convenient spot they were lucky to grab, considering things kicked off in an hour and the square was already filling with townies and tourists.

"Just anxious," Abby admitted.

Bridget grinned. "It will be great. I'm sure of it."

Abby wished she had her sister's confidence, and she *was* getting a little excited, but she couldn't shut out the nagging feeling that it was supposed to be Zach helping her today. Still, she wouldn't turn away her sister's set of hands, especially when making the Harper House Inn's success was a joint effort.

The food trucks were stationed at the front of the green, backing up to the storefronts of Main Street, so they could access their power outlets. There were six in total—including Angie's—Abby noted with a pinch of her mouth, and Dunley's, where Ryan was already setting up.

"Is Emma excited to show Jack around his first Summer Fest?" Abby asked, seeing the hurt that always passed through her sister's face when she saw her ex-husband. Maybe it would always be that way. Maybe you moved on, did the best you could, even found happiness, but it didn't erase the pain that lingered, or the history that couldn't be erased.

You could give in. Or you could keep going.

Abby looked around the green, of what she was a part of today, and made a promise to herself to keep her spirits high. For today at least.

"She is," Bridget said, snapping back to the present. "She's really excited to have a snow cone."

Abby laughed. It was a treat they had all looked forward to once not so long ago. At least it didn't feel like so long ago. But when she stopped and considered all that had happened since then, well... she'd grown up.

The food truck assigned to the Harper House Inn was in a prime location, the sisters were happy to see, right near the kid's corner and at the start of the row, across from The Lantern, of all things.

"Don't go stealing my customers!" Uncle Chip cried out from his window.

Abby laughed. "I didn't know you were signed up!"

"It's Summer Fest!" he shouted, his arms spread wide. "And this is Oyster Bay! Where else would I be?"

Where else would they be, indeed. Abby felt a lump rise up in her throat as she looked from her uncle to her sister, who was already unrolling the sign they'd made (with Emma's help, of course) to hang along the width of the truck. The world might be full of stories and wonder and adventure, but this is where she was needed, and where she was always meant to be. Even if it came with sacrifices.

"Need help unloading the car?" Chip called.

"That would be great," Bridget said, and tossed him the keys, which of course Chip caught effortlessly.

"Thanks for helping me with this," she said as she and Bridget secured the sign.

"Thank *you*," Bridget said. "You're good for business. And I'm happy to help out with the rest, you know."

"I think I'm covered. And if I run into trouble, Chip is right there," Abby said. "You go spend the day with Jack and Emma. They're waiting for you." Sensing Bridget's hesitation, she gave her a gentle push on the shoulders. "I know you like to worry. But you don't have to. I'm good."

And she was good. Or she would be. She was on her way.

"Okay then…" Bridget finally gave her a thumbs-up sign after making Abby swear no less than fifteen times that if she needed help, Bridget's phone was in her hand, awaiting a call.

Abby stepped inside the truck, which had a funky roll-up window, a mini fridge, hot plate, and microwave, along with a few other appliances that she wouldn't need. Soon Chip's tread could be heard on the steps.

"I've got half of it," he said, setting the food storage containers down on the counters. Immediately Abby realized that she'd have to organize everything so it was within arm's reach.

"Thanks, Chip," she said gratefully.

"Hey, I'm family, that's what we're for." He patted her on the back and jogged off to grab the rest of the boxes while Abby propped her menu on the window ledge, feeling a swell of pride.

Not so long ago she was entering the Fall Fest pie

baking contest, daring to put herself out there, and only a few months later, her entire world had changed.

No time for sadness today, she told herself. Today was about reminding herself how far she'd come, and how much was still in front of her.

She leaned out the window, taking in the sights. The volunteers had done a wonderful job with the event, breaking up the town green into sections, hanging colorful balloons and wrapping ribbon from every lamppost. Music was being piped in from speakers that were scattered across the lawn, but by early evening, the band would set up in the gazebo, and the party would go long into the night.

Abby scanned the growing crowd, looking for any sign of Sarah. She'd tried calling her a few times since her last visit to Serenity Hills, but Sarah hadn't called back. Worried, she craned her neck until she could see the kid's corner, and there was Sarah, setting up the water balloon toss.

Checking her watch, Abby determined that she had a few minutes to spare for the sake of a friend and hurried out of the truck and across the grass. She wasn't even ten feet away when she saw the frown on Sarah's face.

"What is it? What's wrong?" she asked as she approached.

"I can't believe I thought it would be different this time," Sarah said miserably.

"Is this about Brad?" Abby asked, wondering what the heck could have transpired in such a short amount of time. "I thought you two really hit it off!"

"He's leaving the paper," Sarah said.

Abby frowned. That was all? "Well, maybe that's for the best. Mixing work with pleasure and all that—"

"No." Sarah was shaking her head. "He's moving. He took a job somewhere else."

"Oh." This was definitely disappointing. Abby set a hand on Sarah's arm. "I'm sorry, Sarah. I know you really liked him."

"I didn't know him that well yet, but I liked…the possibility, you know?" She gave a sheepish smile, clearly in an effort to cheer herself up.

"I understand," Abby said. "Sometimes it's the hope that matters most."

"The only bright side is that they might move me up to a reporter position," Sarah said. "Now that Brad and Zach are both gone."

Gone. So there it was. Confirmation.

"Oh, I'm sorry, Abby, you did know about Zach leaving the paper, right?" Sarah looked so worried that Abby had no choice but to brush a hand through the air.

"Oh, of course. Yeah. I knew."

"Yeah, I heard he went to New York this week."

New York. Of course. Back to his old life, no doubt. His exciting, fulfilling life. She should have known that all that talk about wanting a make a difference was a warning sign. Zach needed to be part of the action. He'd never have been able to settle down here in this quiet coastal community.

Sarah sighed. "And now I'm back at square one. Alone. Terrible at dating. Working the kid's corner all on my own. It wasn't meant to be," she shrugged.

Was there any such thing? For a long time, Abby hadn't thought there was such a thing as fate and all that, but lately, well, lately she had reason to believe that sometimes things had a way of working out, and maybe even a reason not to. After all, if she'd followed Zach, given up her family and this town, would she have been happy? Would she have blamed him the way he said she would have?

When she was honest with herself she knew she would have. She'd chosen Oyster Bay. Her family. This: Summer Fest! And she'd grown here and flourished. And today was proof of that.

"Some things are meant to be. We just don't always see the reason at first," Abby said, wanting to believe that this was true.

Sarah shot her a look. "Since when did you become so philosophical?"

Abby laughed. "What can I say? It's Summer Fest. I have a food truck, thanks to your suggestion. And I have a new friend. And I have...a lot to look forward to." Even if a part of her still ached for what was behind her.

"Drinks this week?" Sarah asked hopefully.

"Definitely," Abby said. She'd need them. She walked back to the food truck, her steps hurried as she approached, making a mental list of everything she would do before the customers started lining up.

There was a rustling sound when she approached the truck, and she rolled her eyes, even though her heart smiled. "Chip," she scolded as she opened the door. "You're supposed to be setting up your stand, not worrying about mine!"

But her smile froze when she saw the man standing in the middle of her food truck, an apron on his waist, holding a container of her scones.

It wasn't Chip. It was Zach.

*

"What are you doing here?" Abby asked, all too aware that her heart was pounding so loudly she was sure that Zach could hear it across the room, which wasn't a room at all. It was a truck. And Zach's presence was all consuming.

"I told you I would be here," Zach said with an amused glint in his eye. He reached for a spatula and held it up awkwardly. The man probably hadn't held a spatula in his entire life. He lived on frozen pizzas and microwavable pizzas when he was in grad school. They both had, curled up on the sofa he'd gotten secondhand when he moved into his apartment, content with bad food and each other.

"You don't need to be here anymore," Abby said tightly. She turned away from him, feeling angry that it was this easy for him, this casual. It had never been casual to her. Not with him.

"Wait," he said, as she walked down the step, back onto the grass. "Where are you going?"

She didn't know where she was going, and for once, she couldn't run. Everything she'd worked for was behind her. Everything she'd dreamed of. Hoped for.

She stopped walking and turned, facing Zach properly, the impact hitting her square in the chest like it always did. A lift, and then an ache. "Why didn't you tell me?"

"Tell you what?" he asked, frowning at her.

"That you're leaving," she said, putting her hands on her hips. When he didn't respond right away, she shook her head, silently cursing herself. "You could have told me, you know."

"That I'm leaving the paper?" He stared at her. "You know that wasn't a fit for me."

"Oh, I know," she laughed, but it came out harsh and unhappy. "Of course a small-town paper wouldn't be enough."

"It's not, it never would have been. And you know that." Zach frowned. "Abby, what is this all about?"

"I know about New York, Zach. About your other *opportunities*."

"Now hold on a moment," Zach said, stepping toward her, but she took a step back. "I don't know what you're talking about."

"I heard you," Abby said, angry at him, angry at herself for still caring. "I heard you talking with Brad last week, right here, when you were setting up chairs. And I just heard all about your new plans from Sarah."

"Sarah doesn't know what she's talking about," Zach said. "And neither do you."

"What are you saying?" Abby said, shaking her head. "That you're staying here? In Oyster Bay?"

"That's exactly what I'm saying," Zach said firmly.

Abby stared at him, feeling the tears sting the back of her eyes as he took another step toward her, and this time, she didn't back away. "I don't understand," she said quietly. She'd heard him talking…and Sarah had just confirmed it.

"Brad is leaving Oyster Bay," Zach said, laughing softly. "I only left the paper. And as for New York…I only went because of you."

"Me?" She blinked, not understanding.

Zach reached up and brushed the single tear from her cheek that had started to fall. His skin was warm, soft, and reassuring. "You know me, Abby, better than anyone else. And you listened. And you made me start thinking, about what I could do, about what was next." He grinned. "I'm going to write a book, about what I've seen, about how it's changed my perspective of the world. And maybe it will change someone else's. I was in New York talking to my old editor. He knows some people in the publishing industry."

"So that's why you didn't call this week." Abby's mind was spinning.

"I wanted to wait and see if it would even work." Zach

reached down and took her hand, and as much as a part of her still wanted to snatch it back, protect herself from the potential hurt, it was oh so much better to give in, and go for it.

"I've gone around the world, Abby. And it brought me right back here. To you."

Now the tears were flowing, strong and steady, and Abby brushed them away, shaking her head. "You'll get bored."

"With you? Never." He squeezed her hand tighter, so tight that she knew that this time, he wasn't letting go. And she didn't want him to. "I'm not running this time. I'm right where I want to be."

She nodded, fiercely, happily, the lump in her throat replacing the ache that had been in her chest for so long.

"I'm not running this time, either," she said, brushing away a tear as he pulled her against his chest, wrapping his arms around her waist.

"Good, 'cause I'm getting tired of chasing you," Zach said with a slow grin as he leaned in to kiss her, right in the center of the festival, for all of Oyster Bay to see.

And yes, there was applause.

Epilogue

It was a sweltering July day, but despite the heat and the heavy fabric of her suit, Mimi looked every bit the part of a blushing bride.

Abby tugged at the waistband of her avocado bridesmaid dress and did a mental calculation of how many hours were left to go before she could slip it off. Given that the cocktail hour had just begun, she figured two would do. There wasn't a sit-down meal, just canapés and cake. And champagne, she thought, reaching for a glass from the drinks table.

"Am I the only one who plans to toss the dress the moment I get home?" Bridget asked, swishing up beside her.

"I was actually thinking of making curtains from it," Margo admitted as she reached for a glass. Nope, not pregnant yet, Abby thought, as she watched her sister take a long sip. It did little to take the flush out of her cheeks.

"Curtains?" Bridget laughed. "Well, then I'll donate mine to the cause." She reached for a glass for herself, and when Abby saw it, a single diamond on a thin platinum band that caught the light and sparkled so magnificently she let out a gasp loud enough to pull Margo's attention from Eddie, who was motioning to her to come dance.

"Are you—" Abby blinked wildly, even though the answer was obvious.

Bridget beamed with happiness. "Jack asked me last night. We already told Emma. I wanted to tell you both in person."

"Another wedding!" Margo cried, reaching in to give Bridget a hug. Abby hovered back, letting her two older sisters have their moment, until Bridget wrestled an arm free and waved her over.

"Get in here, you!" Bridget said, and with a heart that felt like it might burst, Abby did.

"I guess that just leaves you," Margo said with a wink. She nudged her chin across the courtyard, to where Zach was dancing with Emma, letting her stand on his feet for guidance. "What do you think? Think this time it will last?"

Abby looked at Zach and gave a long sigh of contentment. "I think maybe this time it just might."

With that, she picked up what she could of her dress,

the material so thick and heavy that eventually she had to set her glass down to use both hands, and made her way to the man she'd always loved, and tried in vain to forget.

"No comments on the dress," she instructed as he slowed his dance with Emma to a stop.

"Now what comment could I possibly make?" he asked, his eyes glimmering with amusement.

"Maybe that she looks like a big green apple?" Emma suggested, giggling.

"You!" But Abby was laughing, too, as she reached down to give Emma a squeeze. "You did a very good job as the flower girl, Emma."

Emma shrugged. "I've had practice. This is my second time being a flower girl, you know."

Abby knew. And she was about to have a third go, it would seem.

"But this was the first time there was a ring bearer!"

Zach and Abby exchanged a look. Yes, it wasn't every day that the flower girl led an obese cat dressed in a tuxedo by a leash down the aisle. Or that the wedding cake was in fact shaped like Mimi's favorite feline.

"I told you this town wasn't boring," she said, sliding her hand into Zach's. "If you look hard enough, you might even find some stories to report on right here."

"I already have," he said with a sly grin.

Abby frowned at him. "What do you mean?"

Releasing her hand, he reached into the pocket of his sports coat and pulled out a folded piece of paper.

"Tomorrow's news. And my last official assignment at the *Gazette*."

Abby glanced at him quizzically, but unfolded the paper, her mouth spreading into a wide grin as she read. "You reviewed the festival."

"Correction," he said, tapping the paper. "I reviewed the food trucks. Not everyone fared as well as the Harper House Inn, I'm afraid. Those cookies from Angie's... a bit dry."

Abby laughed and read the article from start to finish, her heart soaring at the praise he gave her effort, and her scones. "You didn't have to do this, you know."

"I only reported the truth," he said, reaching for her hand again. "And because I love you. Now, may I have this dance?"

"You mean you're really willing to dance with a big green apple?" Abby laughed.

"I was thinking more like a giant pistachio," he said as he gave her a twirl that admittedly almost made her trip, and then steadied her with his arms. "Or maybe pear. Honeydew?"

"Stop," she swatted him on the chest as they began to sway to the music.

He brushed her cheek with the pad of his thumb. "Or how about just Abby. The girl who almost got away."

"But didn't," she pointed out, thinking of that hard fall on her bike. Her knee was still slightly bruised, all these weeks later.

"Not this time," he said as he leaned in to kiss her.

OLIVIA MILES writes feel-good women's fiction and heartwarming contemporary romance that is best known for her quirky side characters and charming small town settings. She lives just outside Chicago with her husband, young daughter, and two ridiculously pampered pups.

Olivia loves connecting with readers. Please visit her website at www.OliviaMilesBooks.com to learn more.

78967007R00142

Made in the USA
Middletown, DE
06 July 2018